THE FUTURE WE ASK FOR

Archway Publishing books may be ordered through booksellers or by contacting:

Archway Publishing
1663 Liberty Drive
Bloomington, IN 47403
www.archwaypublishing.com
1-(888)-242-5904

Cover inspiration by Nolan Davis

ISBN: 978-1-4808-1444-8 (e)
ISBN: 978-1-4808-1445-5 (sc)
ISBN: 978-1-4808-1443-1 (hc)

Library of Congress Control Number: 2015900020

Print information available on the last page.

Archway Publishing rev. date: 3/10/2015

ACKNOWLEDGMENTS

A Place in the story is the best of positive-vision fiction, inspired for successful achievers.

Inspiration for my novel in seven sequels, *A Place In The Story,* has come from multiple sources, but none greater than from my wife, Mary, and our sons, Charles and Nolan, and their families. Mary, whose own success story continues to inspire her family, has been my devoted supporter and skillful editor. Along with these, there is the continuing influence of having parents who were good people.

The overview nature of my books has come from a list of writers whose books and articles explored the future, advanced knowledge, shared their knowledge base from science and technology, inspired positive insights, and led the way to a knowledge-based faith.

Those who have had a major influence on my thoughts and paradigms include: Norman Vincent Peale, Napoleon Hill, Albert Schweitzer, Og Mandino, Carl Sagan, Norman Cousins, Bill Gates, Fulton Oursler, Dale Carnegie, Theodore Gray, Norman Doidge, Martin E. P. Seligman, Michio Kaku, and others, whose vision is a reference to the future more than to the past.

From these, I have gathered an overarching view of the future. Like an impressionist painting, these provide a bigger picture of our place in the story for new tomorrows and the new sacred.

To: Dr. James Kelly, *james/maria@crx.com*

From: Steve Kelly *stevekelly@crx.com*

Dear Granddad,

Early in my college days, I sent you an email from my college dorm with a special request. I asked if you would be willing to meet with all your grandchildren on the farmhouse porch and tell us the stories you were writing for the book you were writing. I have never forgotten that! The metaphorical stories you told then have become a major backdrop against which I have been trying to live by a knowledge-based faith as I extend my studies in environmental science.

After that, I asked for your help in my work with troubled teens. You responded by completing and sending to me a copy of your little novel, APPLE BLOSSOM TIME.

Now, as I extend my studies, I need your help again. I need to understand my place in the larger context of a faith that respects the wonders of all cosmic molecular existence, and mankind's progressive journey as part of that story. It's a perspective I know you respect, and understand as few others I know.

I understand you are at work on a new book which shares this perspective. Here, then, is the request I respectfully make. Is there some way you could share that with me?

Just as before, I know this is a bold request, but it is written by an admiring grandson. If you can honor such a bold request I would be pleased to have it in any form you would be willing to share it .

I await your response in the hope that, once again, you will say, Yes.

Your grandson,

Steve

From: James Kelly *james/maria@crx.com*

To: Steve Kelly *stevekelly@crx.com*

Dear Steve,

How could a granddad have such a privileged request from a grandson to share his writings yet again? As before, I am honored by your request and gladly respond with, Yes.

I am indeed at work on such a book you referenced in your email. Your request for me to share my writing with you as a backdrop for your environmental sciences studies increases my courage and confidence that I can venture boldly into leading-edge ideas that are of increasing importance in our time, and the future we ask for.

As I think ahead about this, I would like to preface each chapter or section with a note to you, so that it makes it seem like I am sharing my ideas directly with you. So I will do a printout of my writing and notes, then give them to you in person.

Let's meet at the farm house at a time that works with your schedule. Call me on the cell. In contrast to meeting on the porch in the summertime, we can meet in the great room where we can enjoy the unique warmth of heat from a wood stove. We can explore ideas together over a cup of coffee, and snack on some of your grandmother's wonderful cookies.

Granddad

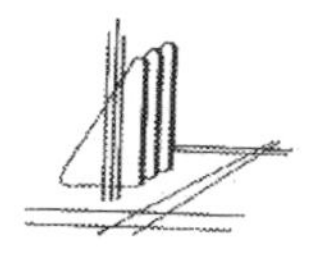

CHAPTER ONE

Updating Proverbs for the Digital-Information-Molecular Age

These are the proverbs of King Solomon of Israel, David's son.
He wrote them to teach his people how to live. Proverbs 1:1

How does one become wise?
The first step is to trust and reverence the Lord. Proverbs 1:7

In our age of science and technology, "reverence" for the sacred must now include a high respect for the progression of knowledge and what we are learning about the oneness of all molecular existence.

We are not hard wired. We are programmable. A major part of our identity is self-chosen. We have choices.

When the Big Ten Universal Qualities are chosen to define whom we are trying to be, they reset the brain to guide our reach for what President Lincoln called, "the better angels of our nature."

Steve

What you read here is both fiction and serious philosophy of life, linked by stories. It is a call from tomorrow more than a reference to yesterday.

Granddad

"ACROSS THE YEARS, I HAVE BECOME INCREASINGLY AWARE OF THREE questions which are of growing importance for our digital-information-molecular age, as we are beginning to realize we are one with the elements of all existence and the unique behavior of their atoms. The three questions are: Who are we? Who can we be? What is our potential? Answers are in process and being formulated into new paradigms. These growing perspectives will rewrite our understanding of who we are and guide our story over the next fifty years as the future we ask for.

We have the greatest chance ever to reshape that future, especially through stories. Everything has a story. Nothing gets left out. Every story is related to every other story in an endless interconnected mysterious oneness, no matter how small, or how large. As a part of the oneness in that ongoing story, what each of us has is, a place in the story.

Back in pre-television days, when radio was king, there was a program, broadcast on Sunday mornings, called, "The Country Church of Hollywood." It portrayed a country preacher and his wife, riding along in their one-horse buggy, on their way to the little white church up on the hillside. When they come to a bridge, the preacher says, 'Whoa, Betsy. Whoa.' When the horse stops, just before they cross the bridge, the preacher says, 'You know, Maggie, I was just thinking. There are a lot of bridges to cross in life, and we never get to some of the best things until we cross bridges. I just think I'll talk about that in my sermon this morning. Yes, that's what I'll do; I'll talk about crossing life's bridges.' The preacher spoke to his horse again, 'Get up, Betsy. We are about to be late for church. I can already hear them singing, "Bringing in the sheaves, bringing in the sheaves, we shall come rejoicing, bringing in the sheaves."'

The people of the white frame church, that my family attended in my boyhood days, gathered faithfully every Sunday morning to study a book they considered sacred. The book told them that the earth was created in six days. They believed it. The book told them that God came down from heaven and took some clay from the earth he had just created, and made a man, then made a woman to be his helpmate. And they believed it. They had been told that the book itself was given by God and that every word in it was true and without error. And they believed that, too.

Near the end of the book, a description was given that told the way the world would come to a cataclysmic end in a great apocalypse, and after that, the good people would go off to heaven, and the bad people would be taken down to hell where they would burn in a lake of fire forever for their sins against God. And the people of the white frame church believed it.

Their children were taught that this was the way the world worked, and that they should believe it, or else God would be angry and punish them. And they believed what they were told, scared to death that if they didn't believe it, they would surely land in hell. Later, however, one of those children gradually discovered, that is not the way it is.

I was that child. As that old worldview began to unravel, I was left searching for better answers to probing questions which arise in our time in history. I was faced with a transforming idea that, while I respect the past, I should have an even greater respect for the future, that the call from tomorrow is greater than rules from yesterday, that what I believe must be reconciled to new revelations from all the schools of knowledge, and that today's prophets of sacred inquiry are as likely to be wearing lab coats as they are to be wearing religious robes. I knew I had to look forward for my identity more than backward. It was time to make a big change - time to cross bridges.

In all sizes of churches - small, medium, tall steeple, or mega churches, in fundamentalist church-run schools, in videos, movies, and religious television programs, unfortunately, boys and girls are still taught that the sacred comes from the past, and that what they believe does not need to square with new knowledge about the universe. The perception given is that the universe is something separate and different from us. But it is not. We are a part of it and it is part of us. There is a oneness of all molecular existence.

In our time in history, we are crossing a bridge. That bridge is across a great divide, from a closed, authority-based religion, informed by mythology, tradition, and sacred texts, over to an open-ended, knowledge-based faith, informed by science, technology, and a future vision defined by the identity markers of the Big Ten Universal Qualities. I have crossed that bridge.

Even though I write in fiction, which sometimes backdrops on real life stories, and often is a presentation of success and self-development philosophy in story form, this open-ended faith I write about is true to life and the progression of knowledge. I was, in fact, one of those children who crossed the bridge to a knowledge-based faith, with respect for the molecular nature of all existence. Even as a boy, I was beginning to know that I needed to have a faith that has integrity with the progression of human knowledge and changing identity, where faith has to do with exploring the future, not defending the past. To use a metaphor out of my farm background, buckets have to hold water.

Some people think we have already crossed that metaphorical bridge to a knowledge-based faith. Some have! Many have not. So, millions of people still go to churches and schools which replicate the white frame church of my boyhood, and are taught to believe in the inerrancy of the book. But when we read some of its conflicting ideas we find ourselves asking if the Bible is a bridge of metaphors from yesterday that we need to cross in order to arrive on new pathways to learning and insights. Even though we may not find agreement with all of the Bible, its metaphors are important and we cannot do without the best of its stories. Those stories are important bridges for building leading-edge paradigms which inspire our vision and build our best dreams.

We remember how Charles Dickens started his *Tale of Two Cities*, "it was the best of times, it was the worst of times." What we know is that for the Bible to be a bridge book, not just for the best or worst of times, but for all times, we must learn to read it, more as metaphor than history, and more as faith than theology. It is time to cross the bridge to a knowledge-based faith that is positive, uplifting faith, and informed by the progression of knowledge and the Big Ten Universal Qualities. It is time to say, "Get up, Betsy. It's time to cross the bridge and join the singing, "Bringing in the sheaves, bringing in the sheaves. We shall come rejoicing, bringing in the sheaves."

Steve,

I am reading across my manuscript again as though I am telling you in person the ideas and thoughts

which define my story and unfolding philosophy of life. Sharing my thoughts as though I am talking to you makes it very special. I am really enjoying it. You are doing me a favor! What I envision my doing all through the book, is to insert sections like this to personalize my story in a kind of grandfatherly, open-ended conversation with you.

I hope you will recognize that in all my writing I seek not to defend the past so much as to define the future, and never to protest against the bad as much as to advocate for the good.

So, Steve, can we be optimistic about the future? Yes.

Why? It's because we are crossing a great divide from an authority-based paradigm of obedience to tradition that has handicapped our human progress, over to a knowledge-based paradigm of personal responsibility for our story. This open-ended approach to life will help us to build our best dreams and give them their best chance to happen.

Why? It's because we are learning more about how the world works and how to work with the way the world works! That is the new sacred.

Why can we be optimistic? It's because we are moving toward a future where we are building a partnership of science and faith, woven together by the humanitarian qualities of the Big Ten Universal Qualities as the future we ask for.

But I am getting ahead of my story. Drop back with me into that early journey of my faith.

Granddad

That old world view of my boyhood began to unravel when I began reading one book in the Bible that was different from all the others. It was the book of *Proverbs.* It had a different view of how things work. In that book, I learned that the best way to live was to look at the real world and discover how it works and work with the way it works so we can make those choices which offer the most benefits and fewest penalties for a good life. The proverbs are not about God's master plan overlaid on humanity, but about how we can make our own plans into wise plans and choices that lead to the best life possible.

The Future We Ask For, is the working title of this book, and is connected to other books by the overarching title of, *A PLACE IN THE STORY.* It is a reflection on my farm-boy faith journey. But it is different because, as a twelve year old boy, I read Solomon's, *Proverbs.* The premise of the book of *Proverbs* is that, we build our wisest life when we look ahead at the consequences of our choices, and make decisions which lead to the wisest and best life we can have. That's sacred. That's the paradigm I discovered as a boy, and the one I seek to extend now, many years later. From those early days to this time, I have read the Bible, not with a focus on theology, but as an exploration of metaphors and open-ended humanitarian faith.

I am not a scientist, but I am enthralled as I read about the explorations of scientific research, with its new technical tools that help us understand how the world works on both the macro and micro realm of all molecular existence. Respect for the mysterious dynamic of molecular existence is a major part of what I call the new sacred. The contrasts between my early farm setting and today's expanded knowledge base in science, is like the contrast between a covered wagon and the newest Cadillac.

Why have I been so interested in the future? It is because I believe there is more before us than behind us, that our failures can be a launch pad for a better tomorrow, and that our story may extend thousands of years into a distant future. As important as it is to preserve and learn from the past, it is even more important to learn from the future because it is in our hands to shape, and our greatest responsibility. So, I keep writing in an attempt to define the next level up for our humanity and how we can reach for it as a personal, life-long quest to learn as we go and shape the future we ask for.

Stories are our best carriers of vision. Ideas embedded in stories reach across time and cultures. We now have the greatest time in history to look both backward and forward through our best stories, for new ways to understand the nature of existence, to redefine our concepts about God, and to build an identity which honors the progression of knowledge. Stories that define identity are like a puzzle. When all the pieces are put together, a larger picture emerges.

For the next fifty years, one of the greatest responsibilities we have, in our pivotal time of unparalleled development, is to make sure we define and model an identity and way of life that is worthy of being extended into the next one thousand years. The heroes of our best future story will be those who honor our highest identity defined by the Big Ten Universal Qualities.

The pressing need now is for heroes who refuse to give up on the dream that we can imagine, design, and build a higher humanity, even in hard times, when it seems like "the impossible dream." What is becoming increasingly evident is that the dream must include a partnership of science and technology with a faith that embraces a world citizen understanding of our time in history and place in the story.

One recent Sunday morning I drove out to the farm. It was cold. The temperature had dropped to well below freezing. The white, two-story farmhouse, where I grew up, is no longer occupied. No one has lived in the farmhouse since my wife and I lived there temporarily while our retirement home was being built twelve miles away. Before that, it had sat empty for several years, following the death of my dad. The house remains furnished pretty much as it was when Mother and Dad lived there. The solid walnut library table in the living room, at which I sit to write, is one my dad had a skilled carpenter to make from walnut trees grown on the farm. I have kept the house up - given it two coats of white paint, painted the roof black, and landscaped it. People drive by the classic farmhouse, encircled by a long wrap-around porch, set among oak trees, flanked by a grove of bamboo, and admire it. Some stop and want to buy it. My standing answer is, 'It's not for sale.'

I went inside that one hundred year old house and built a fire in the stove. I shivered in the cold until it got warm enough for me to begin writing about positive overarching paradigms for the promise of the future. It still wasn't very warm when I sat down at the walnut table and began to write, "These are the proverbs of King Solomon." That's when I thought about a special book. I stopped abruptly. I got up and went upstairs to what we called the 'dark room,' because it had never been finished with wallpaper like the other rooms.

I pulled the chain on the single light bulb fixture and went to the mantle over the fireplace. There, to my pleasure, I found the old book I was looking for, *Hurlbut's Story of the Bible.* It was given to me by my Sunday School teacher, with a note in the front of the book that said, 'For good attendance at Sunday School.' She extended the note by asking me to 'be a good boy and read this book.' I did read the book as a twelve year old country boy. I brought the treasured book downstairs and began to read it again, not only against the backdrop of my story since those cherished days, but against the backdrop of the greatest era of advances in knowledge the world has known.

More and more now, I read against the backdrop of future vision, projected in books like Ray Kurzweil's, *The Singularity Is Near,* in which he presents a promising picture of our potential for a grand and exciting technological future. My perspective, on who we are, is expanded by books, like Carl Sagan's, *Pale Blue Dot,* which take us on a tour of our universe. I am aware of our place in time and space as reflected in changes in earth environment, depicted in books, like Al Gore's book, *An Inconvenient Truth.* My understanding of the nature of our existence, and place in it, is expanded by books like, Theodore Gray's book, *The Elements,* which vividly pictures and describes the one hundred and eighteen known elements of all existence, ourselves included. My perspective is updated by books, like Matt Ridley's book, *The Rational Optimist,* which builds on the premise that we can adapt to changes in the environment, and other factors in our human story, as positive developments in our time in history.

What we are learning from books, like Norman Doidge's book, *The Brain That Changes Itself,* is that the brain rewires itself beyond its genetic base, and thereby expands our capacity to increase knowledge and make choices. What he calls neuroplasticity, refers to how the connecting neurons in the brain can be redirected. As new studies are done on the brain through our instruments of technology, we will learn even more about how the brain works. But what we know already is that the mind is programmable and can create an identity which becomes the framework for how we perceive life and informs the choices we make.

A leading assumption in military training is that the brain can be reprogrammed. From day one of basic training, inductees are expected to accept a new identity, as illustrated when the drill sergeant asks a question and waits for the immediate answer of 'Yes, sir.' 'Can't hear you,' the sergeant says. 'Yes, sir,' the soldier says. 'Can't hear you!' the sergeant says again with impatience, and the soldier repeats emphatically, 'YES SIR!' It's respect for rank, but it's also retraining of the mind.

When our identity is built by using the best of civilization's slowly distilled universal qualities, that becomes a template we can choose to guide us to the best life we can live in whatever our respective age. In the face of the difficulties that may be a part of our story, this template guides our request of life. That is sacred.

One chapter in *Hurlbut's Story of the Bible* tells Solomon's story. It begins by telling how the land of Israel rose to the new era of greatness over which young King Solomon began to rule. Solomon's father, King David, had made him king over a kingdom so expansive that it reached from the Tigris and Euphrates Rivers, in what is now Iraq, to the Nile River in Egypt. Solomon was twenty-two years old. A new era of opportunity lay before him to begin a far less violent and much more rewarding future.

It was time for change - a time for new heroes. Solomon had seen enough of the heroes of violence and ruthless quest for power and expansion. He had seen the weary, dispirited soldiers returning from distant battles of conquest. He had seen the tears and heartbreak of mothers and dads, wives or girlfriends, brothers and sisters, when the ones they loved did not return. He could see the contrast between what was wise and could lead to a good life, and what was foolish and could lead to suffering, disappointment, and failure. As a young man, Solomon may have listened to the heart-breaking war stories of torture and abuse, and wondered, "why?" Perhaps he had stood by that day and watched his father shed tears of disappointment and sorrow, and then retreat to his room in deep anguish, after hearing that his son, Absalom, had been killed in battle. Was this when a new kind of hero began to build in young Solomon's mind? Was this when he began to collect proverbs which point to a new identity, to a more noble hero who makes wise choices for a better future?

In the long progression of the human family's growth in

knowledge and wisdom, *Proverbs* is an early "age of enlightenment" book. It is directly in the middle of the Bible and in a class by itself. Most of the Bible is about people's sense of guilt - about trying to cover the sins of the past and appease God's anger. *Proverbs* is different. It is about the future. It's about choosing one's best thoughts as the way to choose one's best future. It is about reason, honor, and respect for knowledge, about making choices that lead to being a winner at successful living in the midst of an imperfect world. It's about building a better story - about reshaping the future. The recurring premise is that we need to define our identity in terms of tomorrow instead of yesterday - that we can learn about life's best alternatives. Our future is up to us. That is a sacred responsibility. It's the new sacred.

In the beginning of his reign as a very young king, Solomon's search for new identity led him to make his way up to a major worship center and the hilltop altars at Gibeon. He spent the night there and slept before the altar, awaiting insight. In a dream, he stood before God, who told him to ask for anything he wanted and it would be given to him. Solomon responded, "O Lord my God, now you have made me the king instead of my father David, but I am as a little child who doesn't know his way around. And here I am among your own chosen people, a nation so great that there are almost too many people to count. Give me an understanding mind so that I can govern your people well and know the difference between what is right and wrong." (I Kings 3:7 - 9) [1] God was pleased and said, "I'll give you what you asked for! I will give you a wiser mind than anyone else has ever had or ever will have." (I Kings 3:12)

Solomon's dream may have been mostly a projection of his own future, but his image of himself as the leader of a better way to live was a defining moment. It was a new paradigm. Instead

---

[1] Unless otherwise noted, all references are from The Living Bible.

of barging ahead by violent force, human tragedies in wars, then dominance and control, he envisioned his people building a new future through trading and cooperation. It was a choice between yesterday and tomorrow. By doing wise thinking, the future could be better than the past. A new kind of hero was coming alive in his mind.

An old mythological story has a kind of parallel to Solomon's vision of a new level of humanity coming alive. It was the mythological story of Pygmalion, king of Cyprus. Pygmalion was a sculptor. He carefully carved an ivory statue of a beautiful woman and stood back in admiration. She was so beautiful and seemed so real that Pygmalion fell in love with her. He wished she could come alive. So he prayed to the goddess Aphrodite and she made the statue come alive. Pygmalion called her Galatea.

In a different way, Solomon was Pygmalion, the sculptor. His "Galatea" was his young nation. His vision prayer was that, even though his people lived with temptation to give way to dishonesty, greed, and lustful, harmful desires, they would instead, look ahead at likely consequences and come alive to the best life possible. He wrote proverbs which defined humanity at its chosen best. "*I would have you learn this great fact: that a life of doing right is the wisest life there is." (*Proverbs 4:11)

Every Sunday morning of my early life, my parents gathered my two older brothers and me into a thirty-five model Ford car and drove three miles to the big, white, weatherboard, New Home Church, for Sunday School, which was followed once a month by preaching. What I still like to recall about those early years is that my boyhood Sunday school teachers were such kind and caring persons. They may have been fundamentalists, with a theology of a vengeful God, but they were not defined by their theology so much as by a faith that celebrated the human qualities of kindness, courtesy, patience, cordiality, graciousness, and congenial hospitality. Their qualities overarched their religion. They were among my earliest heroes.

At age twelve, my faith became personal and I became a member of that church and began to read the Bible. What part did I read? It was the book of *Proverbs*. It was a collection of King Solomon's proverbs, "discovered and copied by the aids of King Hezekiah of Judah", two hundred years after Solomon's own time in history. *(Proverbs 25:1)* Even though Solomon may not have written all the proverbs in the book himself, he personified the wisest man of his time for defining the best qualities as a basis for making good decisions that lead to positive future benefits. That synthesis of turning thought into little scenarios for projecting the future has become a historic and respected model for learning how to make wise choices. It is reflected in the serious scenario building we do in our time to project alternative futures which help us make our wisest decisions.

Just as King Hezekiah discovered the proverbs of Solomon to be a great source of wisdom, after they had been lost for a long time, so in our time, we are discovering the importance of knowledge, reason, and integrity, after it has been pushed aside for so long by those who claim that an authority-based religion is the only right way.

When I first read Solomon's proverbs as a boy, I thought those proverbs offered a trustworthy guide for living a successful life. I wanted to share those insights for a wise life. I remember one occasion when I took my Uncle Graham's Bible out to the barn, climbed up into an old Model A Ford truck and held that Bible in front of me while I read from *Proverbs*. I pretended to be preaching to an imaginary audience about the wisdom of Solomon's proverbs. Now, here I am at that one hundred-year-old farmhouse where I grew up, three academic degrees and two careers later, writing out words to bridge the wisdom of Solomon's proverbs over into the dynamic expanding knowledge base of the digital-molecular age, as the greatest time in history the human family has ever known, to reach for its best future - to reshape possible!

Across those years, I have read many carefully selected books, many of them not under the umbrella of religion, but providing the same kind of insight for how to live the wise life. As I survey my library now, I can see that many of my books are about science, psychology, self-development, and the future. About one fourth are a kind of extension of the book of Proverbs - books about success and self-development - about choosing a positive identity - about creating visions which signal a successful future.

We are not hard wired. Beyond our DNA, most of our choices are in our own hands. In fact, this ability to override what genetics has given to us is one of the options given to us by our DNA. We are made to make choices. We have never had a greater opportunity to be designers of our own future than in our digital information age of molecular technology. We are crossing a bridge to a new tomorrow, gradually leaving an old age behind. On this new frontier where we are today's explorers, the tools we have at our command are expanding exponentially. What needs to expand along with our new tools is a faith that defines who we are in terms of the qualities we can choose for a higher humanity.

In this new age, when we are explorers with new tools, we are learning that our story is part of the 13.75 billion year history of the universe, the four and a half billion year history of the earth, and the ongoing story of civilization which is advancing in knowledge at an accelerating rate in our time. We are crossing into a new frontier where we have learned about the one hundred and eighteen elements of the periodic table, and are learning about the wonder and marvel of the molecular nature of all existence. Here, we need, more than ever, to be guided by universal defining qualities which lead on to new tomorrows of respect for our home in the cosmos and our own special place in the earth story. We are at that bridge where so much that is good is awaiting for us to say, "Get up, Betsy."

Steve,

I love to tell stories! If my stories can help people choose the Big Ten as their identity framework, I will be more than just a story teller; I will have helped to develop the better side of our humanity and build a better world.

Our best stories are important metaphors for knowing who we are in the progression of the human story, all way the up to the time we are learning about environmental science.

With that kind of objective in mind, read my story about the Queen of Sheba.

Granddad

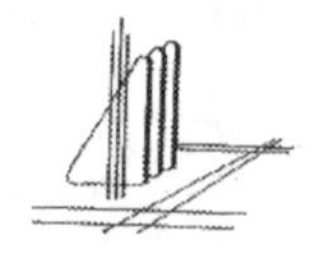

CHAPTER TWO

A Search for Wisdom

Happy is the man who finds wisdom,
and the man who gets understanding,
for the gain from it is better than silver,
and its profit better than gold.
Proverbs 3:13, 14 RSV

"A good name is to be chosen rather than great riches,
and favor is better than silver or gold.
Proverbs 22:1 RSV

To live right, we have to think right.

To build a great future, it is important to signal the mind with positive images.

This is humanity's greatest age of opportunity to build a great future!

Ten Universal Key Qualities lead our most promising future: Kindness, Caring, Honesty, Respect, Collaboration, Tolerance, Integrity, Fairness, Diplomacy, Nobility.

STORIES CAN TAKE US TO FAR AWAY AND LONG AGO. THEY ARE IDEAS lived out on a progression of stages. Some stories extend our best metaphors to new horizons and let us see tomorrow with new insights and greater wisdom. One special story about an unusual visit with King Solomon is told in the book of I Kings. When we add imagination, we can be there to see it unfold.

A guard came rushing into King Solomon's palace dinning room and interrupted his noon meal, anxiously announcing that chariots were approaching in the distance. Solomon got up immediately, rushed out, and stood on the veranda, shaded his eyes with his hand, and looked into the distance, with alarm.

Chariots were the latest development in warfare. Surrounding nations were developing large numbers of chariots. Invasion was always a threat and looming fear. Solomon had built his own army of chariots. They were located at strategic cities on the borders of his kingdom.

But as Solomon watched, it soon became obvious that this was not an invading army. There were too few chariots, and they were moving too slowly. There were only five chariots. Two chariots, side by side, preceded a single center chariot, which was followed by two chariots at the same distance behind. The gold plated passenger box of the center chariot glistened in the sunlight. Three persons were inside. One drove two white horses while another held an umbrella over a person who was obviously a person of distinction. A long caravan of camels, laden with packs, followed the five leading chariots. The procession came to the crest of a hill and stopped. Two trumpeters marched ahead, lifted their trumpets and gave three long piercing sounds to herald their arrival. Then the procession began to move forward again.

As the procession drew nearer, Solomon asked a servant to bring out his crown and royal cloak, so he would be ready to meet the distinguished guest and caravan. The procession proceeded slowly to the edge of the courtyard and stopped. Servants rushed up quickly and laid out carpets before the gold-plated chariot. Trumpets sounded again. A lady stepped down from the chariot onto the carpet and stood in silence. Long black hair highlighted her dark skin and fell on her shoulders. A blue velvet cape draped down to her golden sandals. A guard stepped forward and proudly announced, 'Her Majesty, The Queen of Sheba!'

The Queen of Sheba had arrived from her distant kingdom. Trade missions were becoming popular, but in addition to the camel-caravan being a trade mission, this was also a mission to exchange ideas in a quest for knowledge and wisdom. The Queen had gathered her seers and set out to visit the celebrated young King Solomon. She was ready to meet, in great respect, with the world's most esteemed representative of nobility and wisdom.

Solomon walked up slowly before the queen, took off his crown and handed it to a guard, then knelt on one knee as he reached out to take the queen's hand in a gracious act of welcome. When King Solomon stood, the queen gestured to her servants. They came forward immediately to offer gifts. One servant opened a vial of perfume. Fragrance penetrated the surrounding atmosphere as he waved it from side to side. Another servant opened a small box and unfolded a velvet cloth to reveal precious stones. He bowed and presented them to Solomon. Then three seers came forward bearing scrolls on which they had written the proverbs of the people of Sheba. The queen had heard that Solomon had a collection of proverbs like her own. She had come to share her proverbs and to hear the acclaimed proverbs of King Solomon. Solomon bowed in an act of gratitude, then extended his hand to the queen and escorted her into his grand palace.

After instructing his servants to prepare a state dinner, King Solomon took the Queen of Sheba on a tour of his elaborate palace, his hall of cedar, his temple to his God, and the temples he had built to the gods of religions other than his own. That evening there was a bountiful dinner in the banquet hall with the finest of foods on the table. Servants, dressed in splendid uniforms, served the food and wine.

Following the state dinner in the banquet hall, there was an exchange of proverbs. It was somewhat like a college symposium, with proverbs put forth, followed by questions to which Solomon could respond. It was a brilliant performance. When the queen offered her praise, she said, "Everything I heard in my own country about your wisdom and about the wonderful things going on here is all true. I didn't believe it until I came, but now I have seen it for myself! And really! The half had not been told me! Your wisdom and prosperity are far greater than anything I've ever heard of!" (I Kings 10:6, 7)

In our time, a parallel to the Queen of Sheba's quest for wisdom and knowledge, is represented when distinguished speakers and scholars are invited to university convocations to make presentations. The guest speakers are first introduced with an enumeration of their degrees and distinguished credentials. Their lectures range from science to religion, from economics to politics, in an effort to expand the base of knowledge and understanding. Questions and answers often follow in an exchange of ideas about alternative viewpoints and paradigms.

The search for knowledge has never been greater than in our time, or the search for wisdom more important for our future. All of us now have the high privilege of being informed by leading edge research papers, distinguished speakers, great books, documentaries, and the worldwide digital dissemination of information.

Of course, information alone is not knowledge, and knowledge does not directly equate with wisdom. It is not nearly enough for a guest speaker to point to change, but to define desirable change. So the quest goes on. We all travel a Yellow Brick Road and need to meet the Great Wizard. In our parallel entourage, Straw Man needs a brain. Lion needs courage. And Tin Man needs a heart. And, the human family needs to live by the Big Ten Universal Qualities which help us find our Great Wizard of the future.

The Queen of Sheba has shown up at the doors of our universities, our research labs, our business locations, our schools, our churches in a search for wisdom to take us into a future where we align with the interconnected oneness of our existence. It's here we have our place in the story. We have arrived at a magnificent palace of learning in an age of exploration to design a better future:

- testing whether or not we will advance the great causes for which many before us have sacrificed on our behalf - testing, as Lincoln said, 'that these honored dead shall not have died in vain.'

- testing if we will reshape the future so we can create a oneness of our dreams, and link the potential of our science and technology together with the Big Ten Universal Qualities as our new guide in a parallel with the wisdom of Solomon.

- testing if the Queen of Sheba can hold center stage and say about our plans and dreams for new tomorrows, "the wonderful things going on here are all true. I didn't believe it until I came, but now I have seen it for myself!"

We now have the best chance, ever, to celebrate new proverbs of wisdom, distilled out of civilization's growing knowledge base and evolving qualities. They cannot be mandated by any organization, religion, culture, or government. They are options to be chosen for guidance toward a higher humanity and rewarding life. That infrastructure of guiding identity has now come into special focus in the Big Ten Universal Qualities: the personal qualities of **kindness, caring, honesty,** and **respect,** leading on to the relationship qualities of **collaboration, tolerance, fairness and integrity,** up to the summit qualities of **diplomacy,** and **nobility**.

Day by day we can make these words a chosen part of our identity. We can make them into a pattern we follow in which one of the ten words is chosen as a Word-A-Day quality to guide our identity all during that day. This instruction to the brain makes it into a guidance system that informs our thoughts and our better choices all day long.

These lifting qualities can be chosen by anyone, anywhere, in any culture or nation, whether rich or poor, learned or unlearned. They change the dimension of personal, social, political, and national identity. They define a common ground for dialogue, vision, and planning. They build a climate for peaceful cooperation at a world citizen level. We have the greatest opportunity ever to design who we are, and can become, by these world citizen identity markers.

Living by this identity framework, runs a kind of parallel to being in the Olympics, where champions keep pushing the limits to live up to expectations which are far beyond the ordinary. It's the Solomon thesis - if we want the best life, then we have to choose the identity which makes us winners on tough journey. Does this self-chosen identity require discipline? Does it require great Olympic second effort? There is no end to resetting expectations beyond disappointments - no end to facing new challenges which test resolve. It is a criteria which expects the best for us, but also requires the best from us. It's a tough criteria. And it's easy to give up on these self-imposed requirements. But to those who persist, there is a great future to be built on the other side of bridges we can cross in our digital-information age, leading to the best life there can be.

The Solomon thesis is that, we choose our future out of choices we make from the alternatives we have. Look around you. See the results of good and bad choices. Get smart about your own story.

Make those choices which reward you with a healthy, wholesome, fulfilling, and honorable life. When there are such disastrous results from poor choices - when there is so much tyranny and dehumanization, subservience, and low self-esteem from authority-based paradigms - it is more important than ever to make wise and wholesome knowledge-based choices .

In early proverbs, it was Solomon who talked about this plan ahead strategy for living the best life possible. It's not that hard to figure out what's good for us and what's bad for us. It's good philosophy. It's good economics. It's good psychology. And it's good faith. We can have a faith that is based in our best knowledge to define a great future and make decisions which align with the forces that will lead us there.

It's our tools that now dramatically increase the scale of human potential. And it's the word tools of the Big Ten Universal Qualities that define a desirable future to which these new powers can be directed to lead to our best tomorrow.

The computer is one of our tools that has expanded so many other technologies that make our thought processes that much more important. The computer and camera working in concert is what can measure in micro seconds which horse crosses the finish line first. It's the computer and the camera that can photograph quarks that occur in a millisecond in a particle accelerator, where the search is for the smallest units of existence. It's that same combination of technology that enables the camera on the Hubble Space Telescope to photograph stars, millions of light years away, and send those pictures back to us on earth. It's the multiple advances in the range and scale of our tools that now expand how we think about the nature of existence and our own place in that network. In like manner, it's the Big Ten Universal Qualities, that define us at the highest level of our humanity, and make it possible for us to envision an age when we can, as a real fact, cultivate the higher side of our choices in our information-technology age. In short, the Big Ten form a template of qualities that can actually lead us to our best future, personally and as a world family. It's this convergence of our science and technology linked in a partnership with the Big Ten Universal Qualities that becomes a knowledge-based faith that leads to a better future. That is the new sacred.

The Big Ten Universal Qualities are common-ground qualities which lead to more openness and trust because the motives are not camouflaged in protecting some religious position or political agenda. They are timeless and universal. They do not cancel out self interest, but take our vested self interest to a higher level where we reach for a new oneness on behalf of the common good. They lead the way to a quest to be our best on behalf of the world family. And while that's never easy, it is worth doing in the face of our greatest challenges. We can be proud of every achievement we master. Even better than being a member of the Olympics, this quest to reach our personal level of excellence will bring gold metal rewards and high fulfillment.

The Big Ten Universal Qualities can define a person who is a millionaire, or a person who works for minimum wage. They can define a person at levels of excellence whether or not that person has advanced degrees or little education . These qualities cross all boundaries and can define persons from youth, far down into the golden years. They are simply a continuing reach for the best person one can be in the quest for the next level up.

We can dare to dream our best dreams because dreams lead the way! They release the very energy needed for high achievement. Instead of letting our fears define us at our lower level efforts, our faith can define what we can do at the upper limits of our achievement potential. We can call upon the best of ourselves to step forward. It's our opportunity to taste the fruit of what can be. We have a challenge call from the future. The new expectations we set for ourselves, also reprogram the brain and identity and become our guide to those expectations. Our best dreams not only call to us, they energize the best from us.

We never get as far as our dreams can take us by saying, "I can't." We get there by saying, "I can," and giving our best dreams their best chance to become real.

What is our hope? When millions upon millions choose this surge in energy, and reach for their best dreams, it becomes a collective request of life. Our future hope is that we will we will work together in cooperative networks of individuals, families, foundations, clubs, schools, colleges and universities, research teams, agricultural enterprises, professional service outlets, religious channels of service, governments, and business coalitions, to achieve a new oneness as the earth family. Our hope is that our common-ground infrastructure of qualities will lead us to work together under a large umbrella of oneness as Big Ten world citizens.

When we envision our best future, we dare not look for one single savior, but see the rising tide of millions who follow the service model of enriching our own story by enriching others on their best identity journey. High profile people like Warren Buffet, Oprah Winfrey, President Bill Clinton and Hilary, President Jimmy Carter and Rosalyn, Bill and Melinda Gates, Ted Turner, and so many others, are models of persons who have a talent and financial resource base out of which they invest their time, talent, and wealth to advance great humanitarian causes. But the real support base for this is not just wealth, but caring, generosity, unselfishness, compassion, fairness, - all of the Big Ten - lived out by millions who, one by one, become engaged in those causes which heal the world's hurts and advance the world's capacity to achieve a noble humanity.

One of my favorite mountain excursions is to the Peaks Of Otter in Virginia. They do not compare in scale to the Grand Tetons, but they do measure time in million year units. Of the three peaks there, it's Sharp Top Mountain that displays giant boulders as though they were museum items, perched on a pedestal. Those round, massive, wind-carved stones speak the language of time across billions of years. In comparison, we have only a millisecond to tell our story. But that tiny little tick is of tremendous importance for extending our story which honors the past most by fulfilling the promise of a great future. Like the Queen of Sheba, we are on a journey in search of wisdom.

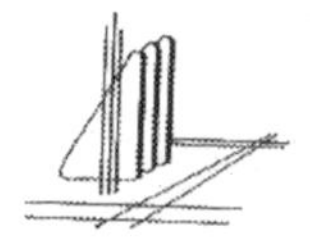

Chapter Three

Temples to the Sacred

"Wisdom is its own reward." Proverbs 9:12

The qualities we live by create their own atmosphere.

Sacred inquiry knows no boundaries in all existence.

Respect for the progression of knowledge is an essential part of a successful life.

Steve,

This upcoming chapter may be especially relevant to your studies in environmental science. It's about the human story and its progression up to our time when we are learning more about the oneness of the earth family and the need for a stewardship understanding of our place in the story. The gifts of many yesterdays have been placed in our hands for building new tomorrows through knowledge, science and

technology, and the Big Ten Universal Qualities. It's the new sacred.

The genius of our time is not that a few know a lot and share it sparingly, but that a lot of people can know a lot and share it extensively. Environmental science is an important part of the expansion of new insights and sharing them extensively.

The range of the impossible keeps shrinking and the range of the possible keeps expanding, and the end is nowhere in sight. What is important is that the possible also reflect wisdom. I want you to know that I am proud of you. Just by requesting to see my most recent writing makes me know that you are one of many who keep expanding the range of the possible linked with a search for wisdom. That search is sacred.

Granddad

I OFTEN GO OUT TO THE FARM HOUSE TO WRITE IN THE ONE HUNDRED year old house where I grew up. It's one of the places where the insight provided by contrast between then and now is vivid. It's where I gain new respect for growing knowledge about the majesty, mystery, and oneness of all existence.

In his book, *Pale Blue Dot,* Carl Sagan highlighted that respect.

> "In some respects science has far surpassed religion in delivering awe. … A religion, old or new, that stressed the magnificence of the Universe as revealed by modern science might be able to draw

> forth reserves of reverence and awe hardly tapped by the conventional faiths. Sooner or later, such a religion will emerge."[2]

Such a time has come when we can "draw forth reserves of reverence and awe hardly tapped by the conventional faiths." Our times call, not for a religion, but for an open-ended faith that overarches religion, so that we may envision a kind of temple of all existence, always open everywhere, for respectful inquiry and reverence. When I walk in the midst of so many of nature's places of wonder and beauty, like in the meadow down on the farm, or Half Dome in Yosemite Park, or when I walk on university campuses, when I visit a great laboratory of science, when I participate in the enterprises of business and industry, and when I utilize the ubiquitous products of science and technology, that's when I become aware of the progression of knowledge and the magnitude of our privileged place in the molecular age. In respect for the grandeur and oneness of all that is, I wrote a simple reflective poem that asks:

WHOSE TEMPLE?

Whose temple is this,
  this field of daisies?
Whose rippling stream,
  sings anthems of praises?
Whose altar is here,
  amid the pines?
Whose sunbeams spire,
  steeples to the sublime?

Whose temple is this,
  this laboratory of science?

---

[2] Carl Sagan. *Pale Blue Dot. P 52*

Whose computers network,
 one world family alliance?
Whose microscopes explore,
 the molecular small?
Whose telescopes glimpse,
 the cosmic all?

Whose temple is this,
 this city skyline?
Whose procession of people,
 brings gifts of hand and mind?
Whose chancel is here,
 amid desks and phones?
Whose plans are prayers,
 to make earth a home?

Whose temple is this,
 this valley of struggle?
Whose mountains to climb,
 echo a call to the noble?
Whose distant new vision,
 is a rising star?
Whose awakened mind,
 begins the journey afar?

Whose temple is this?
 I think I know.
I discovered it long ago,
 down where the daisies grow.
It belongs to the Oneness,
 of the Universe we share,
With doorways open,
 everywhere.

In our time we need an overarching vision which respects the nature and unity of all existence, everywhere - down at the creek, where the water always runs downhill, and out in our universe, where the same laws of physics and chemistry apply relative to their molecular place, not just in our solar system, or our Milky Way, or all the billions of galaxies, but in all cosmic existence. We need a faith which respects the Oneness of all existence that is bigger and more inclusive than all our religions.

Out at the farm, an old metal, beat-up, leaky bucket may hold corn, or even fertilizer, but not water. Our search is for buckets that hold water - for a faith that is credible for an age of science and expanding knowledge and massive data. That faith needs to be such that it not only helps us define who we have become, but who we choose to become for a sustainable future of honor and nobility. I am not alone in this search. So many people are now reaching for our best proverbs to guide all of us in writing the greatest story of discovery ever written in all history. And while people spoof the idea of a utopian life, we are wise if we integrate the best of our universal qualities into our science and technology so that together they lead us as close as we can get to that ideal of a great and wise sustainable human family.

Collaboration needs to be a part of sacred inquiry. Because no one discipline of thought can envision the essence of the processes of existence, we need to work together for crossover insights. This calls for an interchange of insights and ideas among the arts, sciences, humanities, and religion, especially now, as our respective inquiries examine both the macro behavior of cosmic existence, and the micro behavior of elementary particles. As we continue to examine humanity's diverse places in the ongoing story, it may be that religion is beginning to be more open to an expanding knowledge base. Perhaps in these respective arenas of inquiry we can learn from each other's paradigms. As never before, religion can learn from the revelations of science about the God of all molecular existence in an infinite and endless universe. It is an important part of the new sacred.

There are two major paradigms being played out and tested in our time. One of those viewpoints is that one's religion is signaled from a transcendent, spiritual world, above and beyond a material world, as the source of one's beliefs and actions. The other view is immanence and assumes that what we choose to do is up to us and our responsibility, and should be signaled by the best definable qualities which have been refined in the long journey of all existence and the human story.

In the transcendence paradigm, people get rescued from the material world and are given a ticket to a spiritual future paradise beyond this world. In the contrasting paradigm of immanence, each of us is expected to help build a better world here by using the gifts and talents we can add out of our own place in the story.

MODELS OF LEADERSHIP

We can look in on the human journey story and note how some individuals have created highly visible leadership roles at important crossroads in the human story.

Woodrow Wilson led a push for a League of Nations in which we could converge our efforts for a new era beyond wars. In Winston Churchill's story, we see the contrasting viewpoints of Adolph Hitler's attempt to conquer the world, and Mr. Churchill's unyielding persistence to make sure that didn't happen. Franklin D. Roosevelt focused on grass roots economic recovery at a critical time. Harry S. Truman ushered in the atomic era. John F. Kennedy gave the world a Peace Corps understanding of our connectedness, and a dream of going to the moon. Mother Teresa brought our attention to the hurting side of the human journey and embodied the healing effect of compassion in her own story. George Washington Carver multiplied the ways we can maximize our use of the gifts of nature. The Wright Brothers launched us forward in flight to what has now become the space age and landing on the moon. Watson and Crick introduced us to our own DNA with its potential for genetic engineering. Now persons like Bill and Melinda Gates, Richard Branson, Oprah Winfrey, Nicholas Negroponte, Ray Kurzweil, T Boone Pickens, and many, many others, are introducing us to new models of what can be done, by persons of considerable intellectual and financial resources to introduce change in the world and reshape our future.

Picasso and Einstein, each in his own way, held a mirror up before us and required us to see our place in existence in new ways. Now, neither wanting to turn back the clock, or stand still, the hand of time is slowly turning the kaleidoscope so we can see a new age of enlightenment and ubiquitous technology, in terms of what we can do with what we have been given, to build new tomorrows of unparalleled excellence. It's a time when we can give our best dreams their best chance to happen!

We can look back as tourists and visit places where giant steps in human understanding have taken place. There is Newton's cabin in Woolstharpe, England, where his place in the story was the discovery of calculus and universal gravity. We might visit the Patent House in Bern, Switzerland, as a focus for Albert Einstein's discovery of Special Relativity, which took place while he worked there. In an expanded representation, we might go to the stage in Stockholm, Sweden, where those who have made significant discoveries in science are awarded the Nobel Prize. All of these, and their many parallels in our information and molecular age, help to redefine our identity in terms of great new possibilities.

But what about us, who may never be celebrated on any big stage for giant steps? What can we do to make a world that is not just new and different, but better? In our place in the story we can sing, "We are the world," as though it's up to each of us to be a part of a greater whole and do what we can, in our little place in the story, as our place to make dreams come true in the temple we share, with doorways open everywhere.

Those who choose to define themselves by the Big Ten Universal Qualities tend to become more friendly, kind, caring, congenial, cooperative, collaborative, positive, generous, effervescent, outgoing, pleasant-to-be-around, successful, and happy people. These self identifying qualities build confidence and self worth. They add joy to relationships. They just make life more fun, even though these qualities are always lived out by imperfect people in a very imperfect world.

When we define ourselves at the upper levels of our qualities, that identity refocuses the brain so it is less conflicted. These harmonious internal signals create a healing unity and enable the mind to provide positive attitudes and creative, refreshing feelings, resulting in wholesome living. That, in turn, becomes positive image feedback which lifts the mind and emotions to a higher level. When we entertain images of ourselves as living by the Big Ten, this positive vision of our future awakens feelings of hope and confidence. And even if we can test this premise only in our own life-experience and report it only in anecdotes instead of laboratory with many clinical trials, this kind of adaptation and updating of identity in our molecular world is at the heart of the new sacred, and the promise of the future.

These overarching and defining humanitarian qualities cross all boundaries, cultures, and religions, as a common identity, and are embraceable by people of all walks and levels of life, as a personally chosen identity. They model an identity which can be incorporated into the world's educational, religious, and media networks. They will bring personal, social, and economic benefit to all who live by these self-chosen, life-enhancing qualities. Anger, fear, crime, violence, and war will be lessened as the world family finds new levels of unity by living out this self-chosen, quiet, simple, but powerful understanding of ourselves as people of: **Kindness, Caring, Honesty, Respect, Collaboration, Tolerance, Fairness, Integrity, Diplomacy,** and **Nobility**.

NEW PROPHETS

The prophets of old have been joined by new prophets. To think that insights about the nature of god-forces would be open only to religious people is not only presumptuous, and outdated, but lacking in intellectual integrity. These new prophets have discovered new combinations of the elements of existence in the periodic table to create an array of new products. New prophets do research, write books, build schools and businesses, head families, tell stories, use the camera, entrepreneur in new enterprises, and expand inquiry in our macro and micro molecular universe. They join the poet of old who declared, "The heavens are telling the glory of God; they are a marvelous display of his craftsmanship." (Psalm 19:1)

These new prophets of revelation have a kinship with Eve, and dare to taste the fruit of knowledge and inquiry on new testing frontiers. They use telescopes to explore beyond the earth, but also use particle accelerators here on the earth to develop new frontiers of nanotechnology. These new prophets know the nature of existence is both immensely large and immeasurably small, and open to all explorers. They learn about DNA and use computers to map the human genome. They teach the young to use the internet to connect a world of information and build dreams to make this the greatest time in history the world has ever known. They respect the mind and the gifts of civilization's long march toward universal defining qualities. They partner with the prophets of all our generations to stand on holy ground with Moses, Jesus, and Mohamed, Plato, Aristotle, Newton, Galileo, Hubble, Sagan, Neil DeGrasse Tyson, Marvin Minsky, Ray Kurzweil, Martin Seligman, Norman Doidge and a succession of new prophets, whose names may never make it on any marquee, but who know the temples to the sacred have no boundaries in all existence - that doorways of inquiry are always open everywhere. And the procession goes on, as millions and millions open the temple doors and enter to explore, on their own sacred journey.

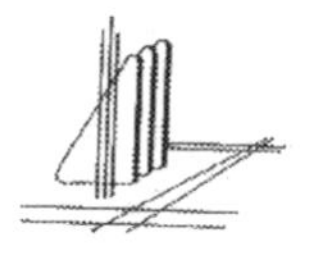

CHAPTER FOUR

Beyond Transcendence

Wisdom and good judgment live together, for wisdom knows where to discover knowledge and understanding. Proverbs 8:12

A man may ruin his chances by his own foolishness and then blame it on the Lord. Proverbs 19:3

Beyond sacred texts, knowledge acquisition and scientific research are adding new understanding to sacred inquiry, possible only now in the age of digital information.

Steve,

As one of the world's leading philosophers, Jesus said, "Moses said unto you... But I say unto you..." There is no doubt, Jesus believed today could be better than yesterday, and tomorrow better than today - that we must not let ourselves be so locked in by the old that we cannot be open to the new. There are

better ways, and it is up to each generation to find ways to be a part of what is new and better.

What I know about both of us is, that we respect the progression of knowledge in the human story, and especially now in our time in history. You are on the growing edge of that openness to the new in your field of environmental science.

Some say that all truth has already been revealed, and must we preserve and protect it. Others say, we are discovering more truth all the time and that it needs to be explored as an ongoing quest, as the new sacred.

In an environmental context, some say, nature must be preserved nearest its natural state. Others say, nature is an expanding gift, never static, and must be extended into a long, long future as a sustainable, carefully shared, partnership. It's all a part of our human story and we are its newest writers. Environmental scientists have a very special place in the story.

I am so pleased that we can be explorers together. So, thanks again for inviting me to share my ideas by way of your reading my working manuscript.

Granddad

I KNOW ABOUT UPHILL AND DOWNHILL. I LEARNED THAT EARLY AS A boy by going down to our garden, down on the branch, and then carrying all the garden products uphill, in buckets, or in a tow sack, three tenths of a mile to our house. I divided those long treks into segments, saying to myself, 'I believe I can make it to the top of the hill,' shift the weight to the other side, and say, 'I think I can make it up to the old log house,' then, 'to the pasture gate.' As I shifted the weight again, I would say, 'up to the old apple tree at the top of the next hill,' until finally, 'to the porch,' where I gladly set my bucket of corn, beans, and tomatoes, or two watermelons in a fertilizer bag, down on the farmhouse porch, with a sense of successful achievement through persistent struggle.

In the long reach for the best rewards of life, uphill is not so bad. In fact, it can be very good and part of the spirit of Eve to risk adventures in newness. But, even amid our excitement about the great uphill potential of our time in history, there are those who say that our earthly journey is never uphill to better things, but downhill to a catastrophic finale which God directs, and over which we have little control, because man is inherently evil and designed to fail. This paradigm, that life is downhill, is a basic tenet of traditional religious views, often called fundamentalism. In literalist thinking about the story of creation in Genesis, the assumption is that we started out good in a Garden of Eden, but went downhill from there because we dared to go beyond transcendent authority - that the story will continue downhill to some personal and worldwide final apocalypse.

As we learn more about the vast dimensions of our place in existence - about quasars, black holes, the collision of stars and galaxies in a billion year time frame - we know cosmic changes may engulf all systems in undefined change over time. In this eventual converging energy of all units of molecular existence, we know we may have only a micro second in that cosmic story. But, of course, that paradigm of the earth story is not the same as the apocalypse that religious doomsday speakers use to alarm people by insisting that time is running out - that God already has the end of our earth story planned as a cataclysmic final judgment.

As we learn more and more about our molecular existence and the probability that the cosmos is endless, that old conventional view is less and less believable, lacks intellectual integrity, and is increasingly seen as fantasy. It's at this point in our inquiry of life and our place in existence, that President Jimmy Carter's, book, *Our Endangered Values*, is helpful in guiding us past the contradictions of fundamentalism and its downhill paradigm of the apocalyptic ending of the earth. President Carter openly tells why he personally pulled away from a major fundamentalist association because of its rejection of women for leadership roles, and it's insistence that all its ministers and college professors pass a kind of litmus test of believing in the inerrancy of the Bible - that it is directly revealed by God and is without error.

It's not true, is it, that the human story is one in which we are all going downhill? That thesis is not in the book of *Proverbs*. In the Solomon thesis, the road is not downhill, but uphill. His proverbs tell us we can be uphill winners - that we can think right and make good uphill decisions - that we are accountable for our place in the story. In that understanding we can continue to learn, grow, and turn old endings into new beginnings.

SCENARIOS

As we think ahead, we can project consequences and see that some choices are just plain bad, and lead to failure and tragedy. So, we just don't go there, especially in our thoughts. We can run personal think-ahead scenarios and choose what is better. The end is not set. Things change. We know that a story which begins bad can end up good. Turning points are anywhere along the way. Any person can discover a superior wisdom and knowledge, sometimes born out of failures and disappointments in the journey itself. It's a view that we can be winners now in our rapidly changing world - that in spite of current problems, our new and growing knowledge base holds tremendous promise for an uphill future worthy of our best dreams. The climb up to a higher intelligence and higher humanity is a future we can ask for! Our own DNA is structured in such a way we can make these choices. We can reshape our future!

The Solomon thesis is not an authority-based, top-down scenario. Instead, good ideas can originate, grow anywhere and be shared so we give our best dreams their best chance to happen, as our highest common denominator. The Solomon thesis is about individuals making choices as their personal responsibility. It's about taking hold of our own steering wheel. This concept of individual accountability can and will generate widespread changes in how we think, live, and collaborate. When millions choose their higher identity, one person at a time, it will have a snowfall effect and build the promise of the future.

How long will it take for the snowfall to cover the mountain? Maybe not as long as we sometimes think when we are discouraged because we become aware of all the wrong around us in our world. Instead, with the progression of knowledge, comes increased potential to choose a future that is better than our past. Each of us has this potential. We can make sure we are doing what we can, even if it is only one snowflake at a time. We can dream and be one who keeps going uphill by putting the past behind us and the future before us, in our nanosecond in the cosmic story!

I know. Some people think we have already moved beyond the fading worldview of the transcendent God of fundamentalism. Some have, but many others still cling to the old identity, with a sense of pride that they are being true to the "faith of our fathers," by holding onto yesterday's paradigms. There are others, who, even though they would never want to be called fundamentalists, still think there is a transcendent God whose word is authority and should not be questioned, especially in terms of sacred texts. And even if they think of sacred texts as metaphorical, some still freeze their metaphors into a rigid systematic theology about God's total control of our destiny as their way of thinking. It's still so prevalent that it is a convenient handle to refer to this way of thinking as fundamentalism.

But many people have indeed moved beyond the transcendent-god paradigm, and live with the freedom provided by the new openness of an immanence view of faith, where both destiny and responsibility are up to us. It is now growing rapidly, as we acquire new knowledge and a molecular understanding of all existence, and respect for the God of the cosmic oneness of molecular order. It's open-ended. It's the new sacred.

Fundamentalists like to read the book of *Revelation,* which projects a kind of science-fiction, apocalyptic, failure-scenario to end the whole human story experiment. They project images of strange beasts, mythological figures riding horses through the air, and of stars falling from heaven on the earth to bring an end to humanity's story. Fear is awakened by imagining a big final battle between good and evil as a catastrophic event. God is depicted as directing it all, as a ruthless, final judge. Of course, in that scenario, God doesn't really win - just draws a compromise with the devil.

Escape for the select few righteous is provided, not in a space vehicle to some other planet, but as a spiritual launch to an ethereal realm of existence. All others? Down they go to judgment, where it's hot. Traditional paradigms advance the theory that God controls everything and planned the experiment from beginning to end, and that it is already set to fail, because the Garden of Eden couple dared to reach beyond restrictions on their fruit tree choices.

When this failed-earth scenario is brought forward to an age of new enlightenment, it can be seen for what it is - an extension of mythology - an early, fatalistic, science-fiction, fantasy scenario, with God taking a few people off to heaven and the rest being punished and tortured forever in the flames of hell. It is a horrendous scenario of a heartless God.

The Bible consists of pre-scientific writings. There is no way its writings are an accurate description of the nature of existence, micro or macro. In those writings, stars are projected to fall on the earth.

But we know now that the nearest star is millions of light years from earth. To claim every word in the Bible is divinely inspired, and a revelation from God, without error, is a blanket dishonesty and a gross disrespect for the progression of knowledge beyond humanity's earliest beginnings. Instead, when ancient texts are read, they should be read as metaphors and story, not as authority from the past imposed on the present or future. Ideas must continually speak for themselves as authentic expressions of existence as understood in the progression of human knowledge. Buckets need to hold water.

In contrast to revelations from God, claimed in religious texts, there is now the unfolding revelation of sacred inquiry through scientific research and other means of knowledge acquisition.

In the days when the Bible was being written, the star-diamonded sky held mystery of the unknown. It still does, especially now that we have a Hubble Telescope, Pioneer II, and Phoenix Lander on Mars, and the robotic spacecraft, Curiosity, digging into Mars soil, giving us new understanding of what planets may be like, and how far away planets and stars are. Out of these explorations, we respect even more the mystery of existence, and ideas about the beginnings of existence, wondering what forces may have been active in whatever began the beginning, and continues this ongoing marvel.

Moving beyond the mystery of beginnings to the marvels of what is real in our experience of life, who among us has not watched a full moon break out between fluffy clouds that sail across the sky and wonder about the grandeur of all things? Young couples in love, still walk along, hand in hand under the stars and moonlight and celebrate the mystery of their time and place in an ongoing, amazing story!

One writer called the Bible the "bedrock of Western culture."[3] While not discounting its importance, the bedrock of Western

[3] Time. April 2, 2007

culture is that knowledge is progressive - that we can learn more about the nature of existence and life - that we can achieve new goals because we have choices and can change the future. It's the new sacred.

So, while we need not disregard the Bible, or set aside its stories and metaphors that add insight, we cannot assume that, because of what the Bible says at some points, God will direct the human story down to a tragic apocalyptic close. The eventual death of the sun, or before that, a change in the earth orbit, making it get so close to the sun that the earth overheats, or so far away it turns to ice, or some other galactic event, might eventually bring the human experiment to a close, but not because God and the devil divide up the human race at the end of a catastrophic journey, as though it were a game.

Activity anywhere in the cosmos may reset activity everywhere else as part of the oneness of all existence and could determine the earth's eventual future. In one view of astronomy, our Milky Way galaxy is moving toward the Andromeda galaxy at about 290,000 miles per hour - and could be on a collision course in a few billion years. But maybe we could delay worrying about that, or any apocalypse, until some time later. For right now, we have some of humanity's most important stories to write. Our own place in the story is one of them.

RETHINKING GOD

Quoting others has not been a big part of my way of trying to communicate insight and understandings. But here, I can do that best by quoting from Carl Sagan. When Dr. Sagan gave the Gifford Lectures at the University of Glasgow and talked about a more inclusive understanding of God, he said,

> Now, it would be wholly foolish to deny the existence of laws of nature. And if that is what we are talking about when we say God, then no one can

> possibly be an atheist, or at least anyone who would profess atheism would have to give a coherent argument about why the laws of nature are inapplicable.
>
> I think he or she would be hard pressed. So with this latter definition of God, we all believe in God.[4]

So, yes, there is a God, with near infinite variations in conceptions and descriptions, and defined by a progression of ideas over the centuries. There are many different connotations when people use the word God to refer to the nature of existence, even to thinking of God as only a projection of our own limited worldview and our changing understanding of the nature of existence. Those of us who embrace a knowledge-based identity, find it helpful to express our belief in the oneness of all existence by using terms like, God of infinite mystery, God of endless galactic space, God of ongoing creation, God of converging force of all existence into an ongoing oneness.

There is a God that links the mystery of whatever causes all molecular existence to be ongoing, billions and billions of years without fatigue, the "Eveready Battery" that keeps on "going and going and going." And, of course, this ongoing nature of molecular existence is what gives us a place in the story. Respect for that in whatever ways we can describe it in our time in the story is sacred!

Of course, even if one chooses to use these as terms, which square better with the knowledge base of our time, that still doesn't answer the question children ask, 'Where did God come from?' They follow a simple linear understanding of logic that something would have had to exist already which could make beginnings happen, even God.

To assume that it took a God to kick off a beginning of existence, also assumes that some forces, such as gravity, which results

---

[4] Carl Sagan. The Varieties of Scientific Experience. The Penguin Press. 2006 p 150

from existence, were already there to generate such a beginning - that there were forces to turn energy into mass. What is plausible to some, is to assume that existence is basic and that there never was a time when there was no existence, whatever its reference point, or form, or density. With children, the assumption may be that if existence had a beginning, there was something there to make it begin. The indefinable mystery is that anything exists, by whatever name we call the nature of existence, or God.

So, what we can do best is to keep discovering what forces are in place, or in process, and learn how to work with those forces so that we define ourselves, not so much in terms of origin, as by the little part we can have in the future of our ongoing story, on our little planet, in our niche in time in history. And that story is up to us and us alone. We, the people of earth, are the writers of that story. It doesn't have to go on forever to be a wonderful world where we choose to live a quality life.

Uphill? All the better!

Steve,

Some people interpret the human story out of a fear paradigm so that it becomes like a drone on a bag pipe, it just goes on and on in its mournful backdrop and muffles the clear sounds of new melodies.

In your environmental science studies, beware of those who keep the bag pipe drones playing a song that defines tomorrow out of fear of tasting apples. Dare instead, to taste the apples anew and keep playing the songs of hope. We dare not give up on humanity's best story, especially at this pivotal age when our potential for building our best story ever, has never been greater!

What I believe is that the future we ask for becomes a powerful request of life – that, one by one, each of us does something that shapes the future.

The environment keeps changing, but the promising thing about that is that we can change too, and can build new tools to help us make the best of the worst and turn old endings into new beginnings of great promise in our niche in the human story. It's the 'I can' paradigm. It's reshaping possible. It's the new sacred. It's where we can dream our best dreams and give them their best chance to happen as the future we ask for.

Granddad

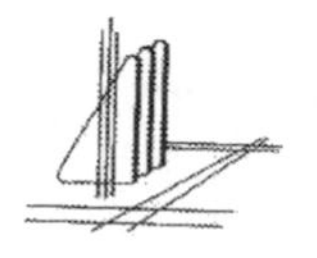

CHAPTER FIVE

A New Look at the Garden Story

Determination to be wise is the first step to being wise. Proverbs 4:7

The wise man looks ahead. Proverbs 14:8

Stories have always been power points. They let us see who we have been, who we are, and who we can be.

Stories are our best carriers of vision.

But, what if no one ever challenged assumptions?

I GREW UP WITH THE STORY OF ADAM AND EVE IN THE GARDEN OF Eden. Didn't we all in the Abrahamic tradition? For many of us, our teachers and artists made the Garden of Eden story so vivid we could almost be there. It's easy for any of us to imagine and visualize Adam and Eve in that mythical, idyllic setting. And, we can imagine them leaving that place of beauty and bliss - even feel sad for them as the gate went closed behind them.

It's time to revisit that old story, but do so with a different set of glasses from the early story teller. The one who first recorded the story thought of the gateway out of Eden as a curse, and as an apocalyptic end of anything good and hopeful, as Chicken Little's, "the sky is falling." Our viewpoint can be far more positive as we look back from the vantage point we have to see the tremendous expansion of human potential, and the unfinished nature of all creation and its molecular base - to see it in terms of new beginnings beyond old endings.

The Garden of Eden - it is valuable story and metaphor. It is not to be read literally, or as history, but as treasured reflections on our early beginning and the ongoing quest to reach beyond needless limitations.

The story begins amid the mysterious wonders of the sun and stars and endless heaven. And yet, the story unfolds quietly in a garden on earth. That story is an answer to questions of existence so profound that a mythological and metaphorical story may be one of the imaginative ways to represent such a beginning. That beginning family has now extended into billions of people. All persons bear some symbolic kinship to those two, and they to all persons. The metaphorical story should be read both ways - they, representing all of us in our early beginnings, and we, representing who they have become - persons who think and make choices and continue to take the risks Eve took to reach out and test the creative edges of knowledge and experience, in what has now become a digital push-button, touch-screen world.

When we come upon the scene, Adam and Eve were hard at work, gathering fruit and vegetables from their new garden, outside Eden. Why were they working outside of what must have been a delightful place to live, just on the other side of that big wall over there? Why all the toil to plant a new garden in this place of new beginning?

Well, it's because God kicked them out of that other garden, closed the gate, and put angels there to stand guard, to make sure they didn't get back into the Garden of Eden. How did the angels get there? And who made the gate? I don't know. Don't even ask. It's a story. It's metaphor. Did they want back in? Maybe not.

One day, much later, in an imaginary extension of the story beyond the old closed garden gate, God came to visit them in their new garden. As God walked along a pathway with the two persons he had made, patches of sunlight spotted the forest floor, highlighting flowers and grasses which bordered the pathway. The path wound its way among the trees, and followed close by a wandering stream of sparkling clear water, trickling its way around rocks and roots before it went silent in reflecting pools. Butterflies fluttered from flower to flower, and the chirping song of birds drifted in the breeze among the canopy of green above the pathway where God and Adam and Eve walked.

Release your imagination even more and you can see Adam step ahead just a little and turn back enough to talk to God. 'God, let us show you how we made one of the pools in the stream larger and deeper. See, here is where we put some stones across the stream to hold back the water and make it deep enough so we could have a place to bathe in the refreshing water. It's so nice to come here after we have been working in the garden all day. Of course, the work is not so bad because the fruit is so good. I hope you won't mind my saying so, but it is equal to any we had while we lived inside the Garden of Eden. And the apples - they are great. We would be pleased to show you some of the trees, and some of the other things we have planted. At times I can't be sure which is better, the garden we left behind, or the garden we are creating here, beyond the gate.'

God smiled in pleasing approval, as they walked on along the pathway in the new garden, outside Eden.

But, why had they been kicked out? Earlier, Adam and Eve lived in a ready-made paradise. They had everything they needed to be happy and content. But they were not content. The boundaries of their minds were endless. It was a serpent who represented Eve's restless discontent. She and Adam had been told they could eat the fruit of any tree in the garden except one. The serpent became the voice of Eve's discontent, and told her that if she ate some of the fruit from that one tree, she would become wise and be like God. Now, Eve wanted to taste the fruit even more! So she tasted the fruit and gave some to Adam. They liked it! But when God came down to walk in the garden, they threw their apple cores away and hid. But God found them and wanted to know why they were hiding. "Have you eaten from the tree you were warned to avoid?" He knew the answer, even before he asked. "Then the Lord said, 'Now that the man has become as we are, knowing good from bad, what if he eats of the fruit of the Tree of Life and lives forever?' So the Lord God banished him forever from the Garden of Eden, and set him out to farm the ground from which he had been taken. Thus God expelled him." (Genesis 3:22 - 24) They couldn't go back. Angels were placed at the gate of the garden to prevent their return.

What kind of gate was it? How tall? What kind of wall was it a part of that Adam and Eve couldn't climb over? Of course, those are not the right questions - it's all metaphor, representing a past they could no longer have and a future they had to make for themselves. They were to live outside Eden. Expelled. Banished. Bad, or good? An end, or a great new beginning?

Obviously we live outside Eden. Life presents each of us a series of outside Eden difficulties to overcome and choices to make. We choose whether we will live with gates in our mind - 'closed gates' behind us, or with 'open gates' before us - choose whether we will live within limiting boundaries, or explore the wonders and marvels of the still unknowns of existence, and be akin to Eve.

ESPLORERS TODAY

Perhaps Eve was wrong in her defiance, but it would have been an even greater wrong never to touch the testing edge of knowledge. She was right in refusing to live on the unexplored side of great possibilities! She was right - there should be higher goals than blissful idleness - there should be a restless discontent which pushes one to cross untested limits, especially when those limits are expressions of subservience and fear. Unless one transgresses those limits, any person will live as a diminished person and unawakened spirit! But, beyond the gate, lies a world of possibilities.

It is important to push back limits. We must never stop within safety-zone boundaries and refuse to explore. That kind of servile surrender stifles all we are and can be. Why do you suppose there was a forbidden tree in the story? Was it there to be defied - to test the limits, not to rules, but to oneself?

Eve wasn't afraid to touch the testing edge - wasn't afraid to venture beyond the boundaries, which, if not crossed, would have become limiting safety zones, imprisoning the mind. She was ready to explore that which could be known for sure only by exploring at the growing edge of experience. The gate was in her mind, and she dared to step beyond the gate.

Eve took risks. She represents today's researchers seeking to know how things really work by exploring the molecular world, on ever smaller scale, in a nanotechnology age. It's here we may hear what God has to say in new words. And so, for all the fields of science and knowledge, they are led by new prophets of revelation.

The human family is not so much 'set' by the beginning couple, as informed by their story about how to live creatively with unexplored possibilities - how to make the best choices in a world of risks, expanding potential, and rewards.

Do we live in a world without consequences? Not at all. Nor will we ever. But often we choose our own consequences - early death by smoking, obesity, unwise eating, careless driving, abuses of alcohol and drugs, conflict in human relations, and reckless choices. The ongoing quest is to live as wisely as we can in a world where there are risks and penalties, but also where the higher goal is to take those risks which advance the higher side of our humanity, where we can create new and better gardens. In the process, we can learn from our life experiences. So, the increasing goal for religion, instead of resisting exploration, is to join hands with science and use its newest tools to help us advance those better goals which make us better people and a better world family. It's a world where we must be real about the problems we face, but also see opportunity.

NEW OUTSIDE EDEN VENTURES!

So, here we are then, outside Eden, free to live on the growing edge of new possibilities. Take a look at where we have arrived in the unfolding human story. Look at the resulting expressions of our relentless quest. Look at our schools and universities. Look at our extensive research centers. Look at one of our newest and largest ever research tools, the Large Hadron Collidor in Switzerland. Take into account the landing of the Phoenix Lander and Curiosity on Mars, 170 million miles away. Consider the satellite links which connect our communication and data. Take a look at our emerging world of collective consciousness focused in the United Nations. Look are the emerging role of our military as re-builders after natural disasters. Celebrate with more than eighty nations in the Olympic games as an example of how we are beginning to see ourselves as one expansive family on all the earth. Look at our developing worldwide systems of communication. Observe our worldwide trade, our banking, our cooperative sharing of earth resources.

TOOLS AND DREAMS

Consider the tools we have that multiply our potential geometrically again and again: satellites that guide, tractors in fields, planes in the air, instruments sent to distant planets, pictures of stars in the universe, digital messages to anyone, anywhere, anytime around the world, vehicles that take us great distances in minutes, computers that direct instruments of medicine and surgery. And we are only in the beginning. It's our tools that expand our potential to work globally and become one earth family, guided by the new word tools of the Big Ten Universal Qualities.

Yes, these belong to utopian dreams, but these are word tools that can take us closest to fulfilling the greatest dreams ever dreamed. Reaching for those dreams is the new sacred mission of the molecular age. As we increase our potential in the digital-electronic-molecular age, we are on the threshold of the greatest age of human history since our representative parents stepped outside Eden. We must continue to step beyond those representative gates so we can have the freedom to match our increasing knowledge and technological power with the vision of a wise humanity informed by our best defining qualities.

For us, outside Eden means using the gifts of the mind and hand expressed in expanding technology. There are problems which go along with new developments, but, even with the challenges, we can change and call upon our new powers to become servants of our greatest vision. Technology is not a curse. Creating new things is not a curse. These extensions of our minds and hands are new tools we can use to make good things happen.

In our own personal development, there are no victories where there are no challenges. There is no growth when we do not push beyond limits. Like Eve, we must take a bite out of the apple - take risks to find our way to new possibilities. It's when we push beyond the mere easy that we find success. So, that's what the retelling of this story is about - it's about affirming success when one's challenges are so great that only those with the daring spirit of Eve believe we can ever find success beyond challenges. And that's why it is important to affirm our faith in our dreams and vision, so we can feel the resulting surge of energy to keep reaching for the next level up!

A PLACE IN THE STORY

Each of us has a place in the story - a time when we have touched down in human history. Whatever that landing point, how good or how bad, we are not the ones who get to choose. So much is chosen for us by our time in history, by someone else, or by circumstances. But what each one of us does get to choose is what we make of it. We can see our landing site in a positive perspective and say, 'This is where I can plant my roots, adapt, learn, grow and develop my skills - where I can use my talents to serve. This may be outside Eden, even far outside Eden, but it's right here that I will still dare to plant a garden. Maybe it's not the best time or place for a garden, but that's all right - this is my time and place. It's here I will make the best of what is and dare to plant the seeds of what ought to be. It's my place to live a great story!'

Who are we? That's what we all decide. In a negative paradigm, and without even thinking of the metaphorical nature of the old garden story, some say we are so locked in by Adam and Eve's transgression that the whole human family inherited a bent, downhill nature, so that we continue to act by our worst inner signals, generation after generation, with no real hope of getting beyond that because, it's in our nature.

Yes, people do terrible things to others and to themselves. They lie, cheat, steal, and kill, but not because they are pre-programmed for failure, or that the environment caused that. People can and do rise above very unfortunate environments, and overcome their worst traits. They make choices. The Adam and Eve story, brought forward to the information age, has to do, not with what may already be pre-programmed, but with what may be re-programmed by personal choice, utilizing increasing knowledge and the tools of technology, combined with humanity's highest and best defining qualities.

Beyond the factors written by our DNA, almost all of our choices in life are open to signals from our self-image and chosen identity signals we send to our own brain. We can set high expectations and rise to a high humanity in spite of tragic life situations. The choice is always there.

Maybe we cannot rewrite our entire DNA, but we can write over it, or around it, or beyond it. We are not hard wired. Douglas Rushkoff, noted speaker, author of, *Program or Be Programmed,* and other writings on media, technology, and culture, calls our attention to this.

> "One of the most widespread realizations accompanying the current renaissance is that a lot of what has been taken for granted as "hardware" is, in fact, "software" capable of being reprogrammed. (People) tend to begin to view everything that was formerly set in stone - from medical practices to the bible - as social constructions subject to revision. [5]

The mind is programmable. That is one of the big paradigms becoming evident as we move forward in nanotechnology and neuroscience in the molecular age.

Identity is a kind of story - a series of incidents, experiences and images, all linked together in the brain to create valuable feedback signals - a kind of guiding oarsman - an inner voice - a talisman - an alter ego - a higher self. The reprogramming of brain activity through visual feedback and chemistry is of increasing interest for scientific research. Beyond that, however, we already know how

[5] Douglas Rushkoff, Open Source Democracy (Demos. 203), 37. (Foresight, Innovation, and Strategy. P 282)

to program the mind and our lives in many ways. We do that by image building - by religion, by education, by media input, by the identity we choose from our social networks. We shape and reshape our identity by self-chosen books, worship, meditation, and therapies, and by intricate selected images. Our image builders include parents, peers, teachers, doctors, ministers, colleagues, friends, media producers, artists, storytellers, writers, and of course, ourselves. We can make those choices which lead to our best tomorrows as we program and reprogram the mind by the reading we choose, by persistent mental signals to ourselves, by choosing universal defining qualities as an infrastructure of ideals toward which we aspire.

We all live in an imperfect world. Many people get kicked out of Eden by wrong and injustice. We get hurt. We hurt ourselves. We make wrong choices. We abuse society's best options. Even so, when we look forward more than backward, and refuse to make closed gates and uphill challenges an excuse for not trying, we can start to work on some kind of new garden. With high expectation and sheer resolve, instead of regret, we can make good come out of bad, turn adversity into opportunity to dream our best dreams, and give them their best chance to be a part of our place in the story.

OPPORTUNITY OUTSIDE EDEN

Outside Eden. That's where we are - always outside Eden. Success outside Eden means seeing the open gate before us instead of the closed gate behind us. It means seeing what we have, instead of what we have lost. It means living on the growing edge of the future, instead of the holding edge of the past. All of life's great achievements take place outside Eden.

Successful living outside Eden means we reach for our universal defining qualities in less than ideal circumstances, sometimes far less, and in the face of real hardships, adversity, injustice, and our own failures. The outside Eden metaphor means we don't give up on our best dreams when gates go closed. In fact, lack of challenge and struggle may even rob us of our best qualities which come out of their cocoon stage only when they are born in struggle.

Part of the achievement is in the reach itself. In the face of struggle and failure, we can learn and generate valuable new insight and energy. And when we fail to measure up to our best qualities, we know what we have failed, not God, but ourselves, and those who walk with us on common journey. But always, out of our disappointment, we can reach again! We know what we must do - get up, brush the dust off, reprogram the mind by the qualities set by our best self-defined benchmarks, and try again in our quest for the best we can yet be in the remaining future. That's success! That's sacred.

We must not discount the importance of where we have arrived as our place in the human story, or complain about the difficulties which may be part of that time and place. Instead of focusing on all that's wrong, and making that an excuse for failure, we can turn that into a challenge opportunity to make the best of the worst, and make new tomorrows out of broken yesterdays.

Maybe the future will be a better time to put together a great life, but we are not there. Maybe the past was a more ideal time to live a courageous, beautiful life, but we are not there. We are here. This is our place in history, our place in the story. This is the only time we will ever have to live a responsible, honorable, wholesome life that honors the promise of the future.

We live at a time when we can choose songs, movies, and stories which keep us reaching for our own best future. Beginning with the home, school, worship, social and cultural networks, education, and entertainment, we now have access to an accumulated knowledge base for developing those values and personal qualities which help us build a wholesome, successful life in an imperfect outside Eden world.

The question for us in our time is not just, 'What can we do?', but 'What should we do?' in order to align our identity with a reach for a quality-based life, where the rewards we seek from life, grow out of what we plan to give to life. Life is precious, not just because it is life, but because we live in the ways that make it precious. That's sacred.

We live at a time when we have become aware of the intensive need to balance our usage of earth resources and the number of people using those resources - the number we take on the earth's resource boat. We are beginning to realize that the lifestyle and greedy appetite of the millions of us who now make up the growing human family, can so overrun the earth's resource base that we place such impossible expectations on Mother Earth that she just cannot carry all of it.

Can we lighten that burden in the next fifty years? The next ten? Can we develop technologies which are less invasive of nature? Can we recycle natural resources and utilize renewable resources? Can we utilize resources more efficiently? Can we develop technologies which use far less earth resources? Can we build an identity that changes our lifestyle so we want less, and therefore, need less? Can we learn how to balance birth rate, health care, food and water supply, and extended life, in a responsible and sustainable relationship to Mother Earth's capacities? Can we move from a pro-life concept of adding as many people to the earth family as chance and choices make possible, over to a pro-quality of life paradigm, where we make those choices which give our best dreams their best chance to come true? It's a way of thinking about who we are - who we want to be - about the future we ask for. It's the new sacred!

The purpose of religion is to help us be better people, not just religious. We do no honor to God, or religious founders, or sacred writings, when we do things in the name of religion which are purely religious, rather than rendering honorable service which creates a better life for all the members of the human family.

BIG DREAMS

While our choice to live by the Big Ten Universal Qualities may seem to be only a 'voice crying in the wilderness,' that defining parallel to the 'kingdom of heaven' dream of Jesus of living as close as we can to utopian dreams, can be a dream big enough to energize us to give our best to life as our request of life, in spite of uphill difficulties that lie along that path to excellence. We dare not let the "kingdom of heaven on earth" dream of Jesus stop with us. The dream of a greater earth family is so big and so important that we need the help of every church, every school, every family, every person to join forces to make it become a dream worthy of our place in the story in our time in history. We have no room for wasted talent. The world family needs the best from all of us. We need all the world's people to have big hearts and caring hands that maximize the good. And while we must choose one by one, the turning-point-need of our time is for millions upon millions to choose to be Big Ten world citizens. That is the dream that needs to be taught in all the learning centers of our world family so we can turn old endings into new beginnings. By this dream, we can be one of millions who dare to reshape the future!

PREAMBLE FOR LEADERS

Those who write our newest Adam and Eve stories, help us define who we are and can become at the upper edge our achievement potential. So, what is our preamble to defining the unfolding story of a higher humanity outside our new Eden as the future we ask for?

We, the image leaders of the world, in order to form a future of hope for all people, will set our identity, defined by those qualities that help the world family write the greatest story it has ever known. We know that often we will have to re-launch the story beyond disasters, tragedies, and broken dreams - that the promise of the future always lies beyond some closed gates. So, we will write our vision story, not just with better science and technology, but aligned with, and by, the higher qualities framed by the Big Ten Universal Qualities. We will define new tomorrows beyond old yesterdays that lead the way to a truly noble humanity on planet earth. As we celebrate the upward climb of the human mind and spirit as a sacred quest in our time in history, we can:

> Sing a song full of the faith that the dark past has taught us;
> Sing a song full of the hope that the present has brought us;
> Facing the rising sun of our new day begun
> Let us march on till victory is won.[6]

Steve,

As I write, I get the feeling that I am back at the farmhouse porch, telling stories of new beginnings to all of you grandchildren, like a few years ago.

This little story that follows is pure metaphor. It didn't just happen once; it keeps on happening for the world's positive people who choose to use life's challenges as steppingstones to new tomorrows. People always need to find ways to replace old endings with new beginnings.

Granddad

The setting sun was shining dimly on Adam and Eve's Kansas farm. The auctioneer's voice had echoed over the loud speakers for more than three hours, seeking the highest bid on combines, drills,

---

[6] James Weldon Johnson

and tractors, and finally, on the lower half of the farm itself. The final 'sold' signal had been given. Many pieces of farm equipment had been bought, and now buyers had begun to load them on their trucks to haul them away. A feeling of sadness penetrated the air. In the silence, the bookkeeper had been adding up the total for the sale, when Adam and the auctioneer walked over together to the bookkeeper's table. "The old green tractor over there, that's the one I started farming with - who bought it?" Adam asked, as he looked at the bookkeeper. But before she could turn back through the sale sheets to find the answer to his question, the auctioneer answered, "Oh, nobody bought it. It wouldn't start, so."

"But it will start," Adam interrupted. "There's a little wire that."

The auctioneer cut in and said, "Well, it doesn't matter anyway. Nobody placed a bid on it. It's still yours."

"And besides, Adam," the bookkeeper added, "you didn't need to sell it. I have tallied up the sale and you have enough to satisfy the mortgage and a little more."

Great as that news was, it was as if Adam barely heard it. He said, "You mean the old tractor didn't sell? It's still mine?"

"That's right," the auctioneer said.

Suddenly Adam turned and began to walk in large, hurried steps toward the house. "Eve!" he called. "Eve, come out here!" She came to the door and down the steps to meet his open arms. He kissed her and said, "You know that old green tractor we started out with - it didn't sell. It's still ours, and half the land. We can start again!"

They put their arms around each other and walked out to the fence surrounding the yard, opened the gate, and walked out to an old apple tree. As they stood beneath the limbs of the tree and looked out across the farm, Adam said, "This is not the end."

Eve tightened her arm around Adam and gazed into the distance. "I know," she said, "It's a new beginning."

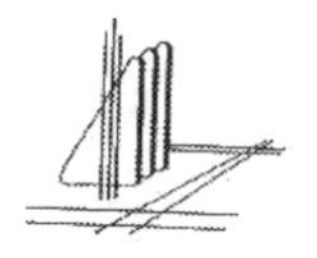

CHAPTER SIX

Paradigm Shift

From a wise mind comes careful and pervasive speech. Proverbs 16:23

Any enterprise is built by wise planning. Proverbs 24:3

You are a poor specimen if you can't stand the pressure of adversity. Proverbs 24:10

When you remove dross from silver, you have sterling. Proverbs 25:4

How can we extend the best from yesterday into new tomorrows?

How can we make the Big Ten qualities real today?

Steve,

This chapter is a backdrop on my philosophical journey story across a great divide. You already know

much of this story, but journey with me as I recall that story. Think of how privileged we are to live in this new age of enlightenment and to live on the knowledge-based side of the great divide. Of course, it's not just a privilege; it's a responsibility. Noblesse Oblige. Nobility obligates. We are carriers of an overarching, qualities-based vision into new tomorrows.

Granddad

I GREW UP IN A PARADIGM THAT WAS VERY DIFFERENT FROM TODAY'S knowledge-based leading-edge visionaries of the future. It was the paradigm of fundamentalism. The people in my boyhood church had that world view. It's not that they were not good people. They were! Their goodness was greater than their theology.

My parents were quality people. When I go out to the farm to do some of my writing, it puts me back into that setting where they were successful in being people of honor and quality-based living. I write in the farmhouse where my grandparents, then my parents lived, and where I grew up. They were highly respected and honorable people. Their story was a test of life's finest qualities lived out in real life in their time in history. Even though their lifestyle was more limited in its choices than today's multiple alternatives, within those choices they modeled what it means to be kind and caring, helpful and honorable people. I am greatly indebted to them. Every son or daughter wants to have parents he/she can be proud of. While not everyone has that kind of heritage, I did. So I can do what the Hebrew commandment said, "Honor your father and mother." (Exodus 20:12)

I went to the church my grandparents had attended and helped to build. My father and mother regularly took their three sons there on Sunday morning. That was where my faith metaphors began - shepherd, king, son, judge, lord, father, savior, etc. What other sources did I have? Like so many, I just absorbed them without question. And that's where I learned that Jesus was a great teacher and friend, and that he had character and integrity.

But I also absorbed the mythological worldview of fundamentalism and its systematic theology, that Jesus was the savior whom God had sent to earth to die for my sins, and that if I believed in him and got saved, I would go to heaven when I died, but if I didn't, I would go to hell. The road parted in two ways at the end of life. As a little boy, the thought of going to hell scared the wits out of me - turned my dreams into nightmares. It was a most unfortunate and very distorted paradigm of how the world works to pass on to a little boy. It was a very limited view of what God might be like, and I didn't get outside that mythological and scary framework enough to see it any differently until a few years later. Even then, it took a while and some disillusionment.

So, I have been through my own paradigm shift. What I have discovered is that the paradigms of fundamentalism are not at all in line with the proverbs of Solomon that I had begun to read as a boy. In contrast to that old view, Solomon's proverbs set forth a very positive vision of the future. Those proverbs provided me with the beginnings of a very different view of how to think and how to make good choices for a successful life. A bridge across a great divide was ready to be crossed.

When I left for college, I had eighty-seven dollars in my pocket. It was the profit earned out of a junior and senior high school poultry business venture that almost failed when market prices dropped. I closed the business out to go to college. I arrived a few days before the fall semester began and moved into a small apartment with my brother, who was already there. The next day, I rode the Blue Goose bus into the city to get a job. I was offered two jobs. Accepting one of those part-time jobs, I went to work with the confidence that I could work hard, manage my money carefully, and pay my own way through college. I did. I not only fully paid my way, I even loaned money to fellow workers, with interest, each week. Solomon's proverbs were a part of my approach to life - see a future I would like to have and take appropriate steps to get there. I already had a head start. I knew how to work.

That first college was a fundamentalist college, but what I soon discovered was that I was not really in step with their paradigms. I had read *Proverbs*. I was beginning to think for myself. I could not fully respect the teachers there, for they were not honest in their thinking. Oh, they would never steel a dime from anyone, but they were not intellectually honest, and that's a serious shortfall. They were so intent on pushing their paradigms about the absolute truth of the Bible - about following the formula for being saved and going to heaven instead of hell, that they didn't really think. In fact, they believed that if you thought too much, especially about science, and relied on your mind too much, you might sin against God, and for that, you might land in hell. Too much science and one was guilty of tasting new forbidden fruit. It was a servile identity - bow down to the authority of the Bible. You don't have to think for yourself, just trust and obey. It was a terrible bondage and oppression of the mind. That old bucket wouldn't hold water.

Fortunately, I was already escaping the mental chains of fundamentalism when I went to another college, after I earned a degree from the first college. At the second college I basked in the sunlight of intellectual freedom. Not only was open-ended thinking possible, it was considered a virtue. The teachings of Jesus were important. His ideals were taken seriously, and people sought to translate them into business, politics, and the ethics of daily life. I respected those people. They had intellectual integrity. They became my new models for who a person could be.

My next venture in learning was seminary. After I graduated from the second college, I went to a seminary at a major university, ready to expand my search for an open-ended faith. What I discovered was not an open-ended search, but an ideology that was in captivity to perpetuating the church and historic traditions. It was not about exploring of a faith which respects the expanding potential of progressive knowledge, aligned with science and technology and great humanitarian qualities which would advance the human family to the next level up in its long march into great tomorrows. The question being asked was not about how to build a great humanity, but about how to build the church. And while that was very good, it was not enough. In our time in the story we need buckets that hold water.

The pressing need for seminaries in our time in history is to project faith forward so it incorporates science and technology, guided by the Big Ten Universal Qualities, which lead to the new sacred and the next wave in a quest to develop those qualities that make us world citizens. If new information has to be screened and filtered through what it does for the advancement of the church, rather than what it does to advance humanity's reach for its next level up, that is a serious shortfall. A true search for knowledge and wisdom has to be independent of religious protectionism or it becomes tainted and biased by whatever spin protective self-interest puts on it. The church doesn't have a very good record in this arena of human thought exploration. In fact, it has been downright dishonest in favor of protecting its own turf, and that's disconcerting to young theologians who want to be respected as interpreters of faith and open-ended explorers of tomorrow, not just defenders of yesterday. We greatly need buckets that hold water!

THE BIG QUESTION.

How can we keep our best dreams from being kidnapped and held hostage by paradigms from old mythologies that distort faith into tools for control of the lives of people? How can we keep our faith from being held in captivity to paradigms so locked in the past that they are no longer build a credible vision of the future? Is there an overarching faith that gives freedom to the greatest dreams in all the human story?

It is important to measure from the future, while we learn from the past. It is important to learn how the world works and then work with the way it works so we can both align with the nature of all existence and define tomorrow by our greatest dreams.

I ventured into seminary with hopes that I could be an explorer of tomorrow, not a defender of yesterday. I wanted to find ways our science and technology could work in a partnership with our best vision for our best future. Unfortunately, that was not what my theological educators wanted for their students, especially for one student whose ideas were defined by to the proverbs of Solomon.

While my seminary had no class that explored great dreams for the future, there was one in systematic theology. In that class, to my disappointment, I ran right back into the fundamentalist paradigm. When I raised a question in class one day, which grew out of my molecular scale understanding of life, saying that, when the body dies the mind dies also, and human consciousness ceases, I became the focus of a very one sided discussion for the next thirty minutes. The professor wanted to make sure he set my thinking straight - in line with systematic theology. I finally said, "I don't want to take up any more class time with this discussion."

But that didn't end the professor's defense. He went on to try to explain his view, that the mind is separate from the brain. It was in line with the dualism of systematic theology, which assumes that body and spirit are separate - that at birth, a spirit enters the body, and at death the spirit leaves the body and the material world, and goes back to God in the spirit world. That is the main premise of Catholic theology and fundamentalism.

The systematic theology my professor wanted so much for me to embrace, is an extension of the two-worlds theory - one spiritual and one material - one eternal and one temporal. In that view, the spiritual is greater and rules over the material. It's the vertical, transcendence paradigm, of God up there, in contrast to the horizontal, immanence paradigm of God down here, in the mystery of the oneness of all molecular existence.

In the transcendence, vertical paradigm, the spiritual is where God lives and rules supreme. From there God, rewards the subservient, who bow to his criteria as defined in ancient texts, but punishes and tortures the offenders who do not comply with the mandates set forth in sacred traditions.

In the horizontal, immanence paradigm, the future story is ours to write. We are accountable. If tomorrow is better than yesterday it will be because we choose it and work to make it happen. That's the focus of the new sacred. Our growing paradigm is that all molecular existence operates by the same laws of physics and chemistry in an ongoing, impartial, convergence and oneness. These laws and forces are so enduring they have been the operating base of the universe for more than thirteen billion years, and so precise that astronomers know when a total eclipse of the moon will occur, to the hour and minute. Learning how the world works, then, working with the way the world works is the new sacred.

People who recognize the molecular nature of existence realize that whatever our understanding of the nature of God has been, and continues to be, it must be in alignment with the ongoing and impartial 13.75 billion years of molecular forces. What we are now realizing is that the progression of knowledge and its new tools of science, technology, and engineering are revealing a growing understanding of God, where we may now, "draw forth reserves of reverence and awe hardly tapped by the conventional faiths." [7] In this freedom, there is trust and respect for the impartial God of all the micro and macro forces of existence. It is a higher sense of reverence, and leads to respect for our place in the cosmic story.

---

[7] Carl Sagan. *Pale Blue Dot. P 52*

In spite of this paradigm shift, the subtle disguised premise of fundamentalism continues, and follows a kind of *quid pro quo* paradigm in which a reward is expected in exchange for obedience and praise of the God, up there. It is disguised in the claims that God is love, when, in fact, the concept of a God who punishes people for their sins eternally, totally betrays that premise, and can never be thought of as a God who is just and good. So, do people still believe this contradictory paradigm in our time? They do, indeed. Millions do. It's a basic premise in many religions of the world, even though it comes out of a "dark ages" paradigm of guilt, fear, and control over people. It is a paradigm of subservience to a transcendent God. People bow down to this God as an obsession, whatever its varying expressions may take in different religions. God is thought of as someone to be obeyed and worshiped, instead of being expressed in the underlying forces operative in all existence.

In the Christian fundamentalist orientation, people wave their arms in the air as they praise God and sing, "God is so good," in a form of praise and flattery, in a *quid pro quo* expectation that God will favor them for their praise, and, in turn, will bless their lives now, and especially at the end of life. It is a kind of bargain with God. It assumes God runs the world on a rewards and punishment basis. If you please God, you will be rewarded. If not, you will be punished, and that severely. Forever. It's a formula. You don't have to think, just follow the formula - align with tradition and systematic theology. The premise is that it is all spelled out in the Bible and you must believe it and go by it to be okay with God. If you don't, you are in trouble with God, and "God don't take no crap." You gotta pay up, or find forgiveness. Else, you know what, God will let Satan take over and do his "dirty work" for him, and keep you in his fire box forever.

But, of course, in their theological formula of how God has it all fixed, you can escape such a bad end and be taken up to heaven as a reward, with a mansion all your own, just by getting into good graces with God. But, while the good guys are in heaven and praising God all day long, can you imagine the bad guys in hell lifting their arms in praise of the love of God and singing, "God is so good?" It's all such an absurd and contradictory paradigm!

That formula is not in the book of *Proverbs*. And it should never be taught in any seminary class on systematic theology as an understanding of how the world works. But it is, and some people buy into this theology as the truth about the way things are. They never see how the progression of knowledge, developed in the lengthening human journey, should change the way we understand God, existence, and faith. The fundamentalist world view belongs with the old pre-Columbus view, "the world is flat", and is not only a contradiction of reason and progressive knowledge, it is dishonest and a lack of intellectual integrity.

More and more people are seeing through the contradictions of this old paradigm, with its empty promises and ethereal based paradigms. They are beginning to understand the nature of existence in terms of the oneness of the behavior of all the elements which make up the one hundred and eighteen elements of existence, and which operate by the same dynamic forces everywhere in all micro and macro existence. Many people are beginning to see the contrasts between, a religion based in the assumption that there is a spirit world, and a faith that is based in a growing knowledge about the oneness of the molecular world of existence as we have come to know it in our time of progressive knowledge.

In the knowledge-based view, knowledge is progressive. We learn forward. We learn as we go, and the doorway of knowledge is continually opening wider and wider as a sacred inquiry, especially in our time of research in science and technology, with its advanced instruments of inquiry and awareness.

People who follow Solomon's train of thought just don't buy into the old paradigm which makes God out as the grand designer of a predetermined, downhill, failed plan for humanity. In the Solomon thesis, our sins are not against God, but against ourselves. We are both the offender and the offended. We infringe on our own rewards. We go against our own best interests. Our sins are against our best developing story and its future possibilities. It's here that we can turn things around by the choices we make by the qualities we choose that guide and develop our own best story.

So, I'm with Solomon. I can easily do without systematic theology. The premise I raised in the discussion with my seminary professor is not so bad - believing that one's lifetime story is one's responsibility and one's immortality - that when we die, we lose consciousness and that's the end of the journey. Eternal life is not necessary, or even desired. It is enough to have lived and marched as part of the incredible journey of human civilization on planet earth, in our time in history. And the story goes on.

A CREDIBLE FAITH

Across the centuries, religion has tried to figure out how to beat death. But nobody beats death. It's not even desirable. It's just not the name of the game. In fact, the idea that people live forever as spirits is one of religion's most cruel paradigms. On the other hand, one of the most consoling ideas one can have about the end of life is just that, that it ends. We don't have to worry about being dead. Consciousness ceases. We won't even know we are dead. The molecular interaction of all existence continues on in new convergence, and old endings become new beginnings of whatever state particles may take. And we won't have to worry about living for a billion years, or even a million, or "ten thousand." If we did, in fact, go to heaven to meet all our "dear loved ones again," it might not be all that much of a heaven, when we discover that so and so is not there, and if not, then God must have let the devil have that person to take down into eternal captivity - must have gone to hell. So, who could enjoy being in heaven with God, when he has sent so many others, including our "dear loved ones," down to be tortured forever in the fiery furnace?

As I say, it's a cruel, cruel paradigm. So one of the best things about life is that it ends. All consciousness ceases. Everyone can finally say "Goodbye" and leave the future to the future, and to succeeding generations. That's a very consoling idea. One's own story converges into the progressive and continuing story of humanity, into the story of the earth, the solar system, the universe, and the ongoing activity of all molecular existence whatever its form or density. What each of us has is simply a place in the story.

Colleges and universities across the world are among our most significant leaders of the future. Universities have become major research centers which explore the nature of existence. They have a major responsibility to lead the way to make this the greatest age in history that the world has ever known, and to make the vision of a better future an integral part of the university's mission and curriculum. The promise of the future is enhanced by the uplifting towers and green quadrangles of our college and university campuses. They are inspiring symbols of exploring the future as an open and sacred inquiry. Students who walk on those campus walkways are at the growing edge of their search for dreams and identity. They deserve an education in sync with our best knowledge which makes them ready to cross bridges to new frontiers of a knowledge-based faith.

Professors in any classroom have a strategic opportunity to build the vision of a great future. With quiet, open, honest words, they can give students glimpses into a tomorrow defined by the long progression of civilization's slowly distilled qualities of **kindness, caring, honesty,** and **respect,** leading on to **collaboration, tolerance, fairness,** and **integrity,** and the summit qualities of **diplomacy, and nobility**. One by one, today's students can expand the best gifts of civilization through their own insights and talent base and by making the Big Ten Universal Qualities the markers by which they live out their part in the greatest dreams of the human story.

But, of course, the two-worlds paradigm continues. In funeral services, ministers read the twenty-third Psalm, where the assumption is that a "shepherd" in the spirit world is watching over people in the material world, leading them "beside still waters." But there is so much in real life experience which indicates that neither God or angels provide that kind of "still waters" protection and exemption from tragedy, disaster, and wrong. Even so, the psalm ends with people escaping life's troubles by being translated from the material to the spiritual, up to, or out to, where God lives. The closing metaphor says, "I shall dwell in the house of the Lord forever."

While finding a full understanding of ultimate reality escapes both science and religion, belief systems that take account of the molecular nature of all existence is a faith for which we are accountable. This is the main assumption recurring in the proverbs of Solomon and the underlying premise of the new sacred - that the future is up to us, and is created by the thoughts we think and the choices we make, aligned with the mysterious oneness of our place in all molecular existence.

All too often, a funeral service projects a future no one knows about for sure, and, in the meantime, fails to be a memorial service to honor the real time human story. A funeral service is an opportunity to give a tribute to the way a person may have been guided by "whatever is true, whatever is honorable, whatever is just, whatever is pure, whatever is lovely, whatever is gracious, if there is any excellence, if there is anything worthy of praise, think about these things." (Philippians 4:8 RSV)

A funeral service need not be a passport to another world beyond light speed, but a simple and honest farewell tribute to one person's life story as it has been lived, and now completed, as one story in humanity's succession of stories.

A memorial service is a time to celebrate the good in a person's story that has added to the progression of civilization's slowly refined Big Ten Universal Qualities. It is a time to recall the story of those whose names belong in the "wise man's hall of fame." It is a time to quote from Longfellow's, *A Psalm of Life*,

> Lives of great men all remind us
> We can make our lives sublime.
> And, departing, leave behind us
> Footprints on the sands of time.[8]

Steve,

If you wonder why all this is relevant to a student in environmental science, it's because of the need to learn how the world works and how we can work with the way the world works so that the end game is to build a better world. We live in that very special time and promising era when scientists, business leaders, social planners, religious leaders, educators, military, leaders in government, and many other career and professional channels of service, all need to find answers to the same question, 'How can we build a tomorrow worthy of our time and place in the greatest time in the human story?'

What I have talked about as simply as I know how, is relevant because, as never before, the focus must not be on what God will do for us, but on what we will do for ourselves to create a better future as a measure of our responsibility.

Granddad

[8] Longfellow. *A Psalm of Life*

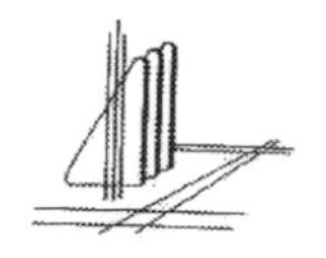

Chapter Seven

Principles of Problem Solving

He who loves wisdom loves his own best interest and will be a success. Proverbs 19:8

It is possible to give away and become richer! It is also possible to hold on too tightly and lose everything.
Yes, the liberal man shall be rich! By watering others he waters himself. Proverbs 11:24, 25

Don't you know that this good man, though you trip him up seven times, will each time rise again? Proverbs 24:16

If you profit from constructive criticism you will be elected to the wise man's hall of fame. Proverbs 15:31

**There is no reason not to build big dreams
in the face of big challenges.
Especially then it is true,
that what we plan to give to life
becomes our request of life.**

**If the best we have, is all we have,
we must make the most of it.**

**Ten Principles of Problem Solving lead the way
to turn problems into opportunity.**

Steve,

Sooner or later, all of us run into challenges where we need to know the Principles of Problem Solving. I believe in these principles and use them as valuable "proverbs" for our time. I keep trying to be informed by them day by day, especially when I hit some of life's tough places.

Granddad

WHEN I HEARD ITZHAK PERLMAN PERFORM BEETHOVEN'S "VIOLIN Concerto in D" with a noted orchestra, I thought, *that is the most beautiful music I have ever heard.* The next day I purchased a CD of Mr Perlman's recording of Beethoven's concerto. Since then I have played it many, many times. I sometimes lie on the carpet, in front of the stereo, and absorb its dynamic harmonies and recurring themes.

For that great music, we are first indebted to Beethoven, who triumphed over adversity and kept on creating great music even while he was becoming deaf. But this performance of Beethoven's great music was a gift of excellence created out of Itzhak Pearlman's triumph over adversity. When he was four years old, he contracted the crippling disease of polio. He learned to walk with the aid of crutches. With that kind of debilitating handicap, what kind of success could a little boy create? He excelled by learning to play a violin. Now he is celebrated as one of the greatest violinists of all time. When he walks on stage, it is laboriously with the aid of two crutches. He plays while seated. The scale of his achievement in the face of enormous challenge can be illustrated by his appearance and performance at a White House State Dinner in honor of Her Majesty, Queen Elizabeth II.

His achievement is an example of how adversities, heroically encountered, can become stepping-stones to a higher level of achievement, which would not have been possible if there had been no difficulties to overcome.

Research in neurological science is giving us new insight into how the brain works. What is clearly established is that input to the brain, signals emotions and behavior, and the intentional selection of right thoughts and images can guide one to a wise life. That is the recurring theme of Solomon's proverbs - think success and it will lead to success. The book of *Proverbs* is very different from other parts of the Bible where the emphasis is on what God can do for us. *Proverbs* is about what we can do for ourselves. It's about thinking right thoughts. It's about taking responsibility for our own story. It's about reshaping the future!

Solomon was a "success and self-development" writer for his time. When we sequence his proverbs forward to our time, we hear parallels to Solomon's positive advice at the Success Motivation Rallies we attend. Likewise, many books reflect the same approach, with the thesis of think and grow successful; input the mind with positive thoughts, especially in the face of struggle and adversity - create a winning state of mind. All of us can generate vital new energy when we announce to and for ourselves, that we will be winners in life in spite of hardship, struggle, injustice, or failures. Challenge, even failure, can be our best teachers, helping us to learn how to turn old endings into new beginnings. One successful businessman said, "To get wisdom you have to live through a lot of mistakes. You can't skip these stages." And so we struggle with our failures and disappointments until finally, we get it - that some of our best opportunities develop while we learn and grow through our struggles and challenges. Therefore, we understand Solomon's question, "*Don't you know that the good man, though you trip him up seven times, will each time rise again?*"

We live at a time when the potential to build great tomorrows beyond failed yesterdays has never been greater. We may know of persons who have achieved success because they dared to keep on giving positive signals to their minds in the face of major challenges. Rich or poor, known or unknown, they became winners and new heroes.

Life is not always easy. Sometimes it's tough! The news is not always good. We may get news that we have a major illness and have to face that new reality. We may learn about the loss of our loved ones. War sometimes brings tragic news with a knock on our front door, making it necessary to go on beyond broken dreams, even though it hurts, and keeps on hurting. People say things that hurt. Relationships go bad. Families break up. Financial struggles come along. Storms destroy homes, businesses, and crops. Some people have to deal with cruelty and injustice. Loss of a job, or low income, makes it hard for some families. Some children have it tough at home and school. Some teenagers are caught in really bad and embarrassing situations where they are not respected as real persons. Sooner or later, we all know something about bad news and tough journey. But when the worst happens, that is when we are tested for our ability to make the best out of the worst and to turn struggle into triumph.

In the face of tough journey, the mind has a resilient ability to reprogram itself when it is signaled by the input of positive expectations. We all face instances when it is very important to use that ability to reprogram our own mind.

There are so many failed dreams in our time. Young people set out with dreams of putting together a great life. Then come war and tragedy. Then come accidents. Friends and family members are disabled or killed. Sickness and disease. Crime. Drugs. Prison. Sexual offenses. Consequences of unwise choices. Politics in the work place. Favoritism. Unfairness. Company layoffs. There is so much disappointment, disillusionment, hurt, embarrassment, distrust, loss of respect, anger, resentment, and fear. Sooner or later everyone needs to survive the tough places. No one is exempt. But we can win again beyond loss. The Olympic flame goes out, but not the Olympic spirit. We all need new proverb-updates which reprogram the mind and signal our choices for new tomorrows beyond old yesterdays.

The book of *Proverbs* is that kind of "how to win" book - a gathering of hundreds of bits of advice about solving problems. I have personally referred to the proverbs many times, and found them to be helpful in bringing my best thinking to bear on my toughest moments.

Out of my personal struggle-to-triumph journey, and with the proverbs of Solomon as a backdrop, I have created Ten Principles of Problem Solving which become updated proverbs for our time. These principles of problem solving are little capsules of insight we can use to enter a request to our brain for its guidance to help us turn old endings into new beginnings.

One young realtor, who cherished her copy of these principles said, "When I hit a tough spot, I open my desk drawer and pull them out, and read them again." Even though I wrote them, I still recall them, or bring them out and read them, when I need to be absolutely sure that I am doing positive, winning thinking which resets my emotions, heals my attitudes, and guides my choices.

Each time we read these, "new proverbs," we will be at a different place in our story, so each time they will speak to us with new insights. Because of this, we need to read them again and again in our reach to give our best dreams their best chance to happen.

TEN PRINCIPLES OF PROBLEM SOLVING

1. MAKE SURE YOU ARE WORKING ON THE FUTURE INSTEAD OF MERELY FRETTING ABOUT THE PAST. When things get broken, fix them, if possible, or important, or even wise, then move on to make new beginnings beyond old endings. Put the past behind you and the future before you, just as much as you possibly can. Don't just live with your mistakes, live beyond them. When you make a mistake, correct it, if possible, or wise, then be sure you turn loose of the past, with its guilt, so you can take hold of the future. Learn from your disappointments, mistakes, and failures, then move ahead by building and repeating affirmations about your new and wiser future in which you will make something good come out of your challenges. All of us must ask ourselves again and again, "Is what I am thinking and planning, about the past, or about my best future?"

2. IMAGINE THE BEST THAT CAN HAPPEN. Feed in positive thoughts! They may, or may not, be directly related to the crisis at hand, but those positive thoughts release creative forces in the mind which carry over into whatever it is for which you need positive energy. Instead of saying, "I can't, and this is the end," release valuable energy by saying, "I can, and this is a new beginning."

3. MAXIMIZE and **MINIMIZE**. As the song goes, "Accentuate the positive, Eliminate the negative." Add to the good and reduce the bad. Make the most of what you have. Instead of bemoaning what you have lost, or don't have, make sure you are taking maximum advantage of what you do have, and can yet achieve. So what, other people are smarter or better positioned, go ahead and make a success of life anyway, the way you can, with your skills and your place in life. So what, someone else didn't do things like they should, or you made mistakes, that's no reason to give up in surrender. Instead, it's your opportunity to give even more. Talk tough to yourself. Set demanding expectations. Make extra effort. Go the extra mile. Keep on giving. Write your best story. It will not be perfect, but it will be your best, and you can be proud of it.

Remember, it's your story and you can't un-write it, but you can write the next chapter better, by learning from experience. Make it as good as you can for yourself and others by looking ahead and choosing what is worthy of your maximum effort.

4. LIVE BEYOND YOUR PROBLEMS. Some problems will never go away Some are not in your control. The choice you have is to adjust to them, and keep on adjusting, learn from them, detour around, live triumphantly with and beyond them, and succeed in spite of them.

Life is not always easy. Sometimes it is tough, and you may have to change modes and do big attitude resets in order to stay flexible and be gracious. That's when it may be necessary to look for ways to make the best of the worst and use the hard places to test how nearly you can live up to the Big Ten Universal Qualities

Keep the future open. Envision new plans for your future. Figure out the best way to go on from here. There are positive ways to deal with negative situations. In short, learn to make the best of the worst, and the most of the least. Easy? No. But hard is not a reason for not doing something. Life goes on. Leave as much of the bad as you can behind, and put as much of the good as you can before you.

5. LOOK FOR THE OPPORTUNITY IN YOUR PROBLEM. Not all difficulties you face, even extreme challenges, will be against you - some will bring greater opportunity for enriched fulfillment and success if you learn, grow, and become more positive and authentic in the face of the problem. Look for the good, even in the bad, and look for ways to make good come out of the bad. The challenges you face may release and bring out the butterfly from its cocoon existence.

6. MAKE YOUR BEST DECISION, AND THEN WORK TO MAKE THE DECISION RIGHT. Even the best decision will not be good enough unless you work to make it into a continuing good decision. And, even a poor decision can be turned into a good decision if you work to make good come out of it. A story that begins bad can end up good. There are new beginning points all along the way.

Sometimes we get "bumped" by harsh, un-chosen circumstances into new beginnings which have the potential to become great opportunity, if we keep signaling our mind and emotions with positive thoughts.

7. THINK SUCCESS! Believe that special, exciting, creative forces will energize you to perform at new levels of confidence, power, and excellence while you are thinking of success. Refuse to think fear thoughts. Fear makes problems seem bigger than they are. Break your problems down into manageable units and then address them with an, "I can," frame of mind. That way, when the new opportunities come, you will address them out of the positive energy awakened by your best thoughts.

8. GIVE YOUR FINEST EFFORT INTO LIFE WHERE YOU ARE, NO MATTER WHAT YOU ARE FACING. You will make mistakes and have to face consequences. People will be bad to you and you will be disadvantaged or hurt. Still, and even more then, require of yourself that you give the best you have to life. That effort may not change the past, but it can change the future.

9. CHANGE THE FOCUS OF YOUR LIFE FROM SELF TO OTHERS. Self absorption does not solve problems.

Find ways to make life more pleasant and fun for both yourself and others as your leading identity. Believe the old song, "Make someone else happy and you will be happy, too." It's true, as Mary Poppins said, "In everything to be done, there is an element of fun." Find it. Happiness is a by-product - it comes when you give it away. Learn to laugh at more things. Be congenial and pleasant so that others will like to be around you. Be nice to those who are not nice to you. Give away some act or word of kindness at every opportunity. Still be friends with others who have different opinions. Do the big and generous thing, and do it first. You be the one who gives. Restate the golden rule - "I will give unto others the joy I would like to receive." Make life real fun!

10. PERSIST. Keep your best dreams alive. Keep trying. Do not give up on worthy goals. We win only if we are still in there playing the game. Reflect on yesterday but envision tomorrow. Trust the positive, energizing dynamic set forth in the dependable axiom of Jesus, "While you are asking, it will be given you; while you are seeking, you will find; and while you are knocking, it will be opened to you." (Matt. 7:7 Literal translation from Greek) There are opportunities you don't see until you are looking for them.

Your mind is your server. You reset the brain when you tell your brain who you want to be and what you plan to give to life. Out of that signal, it goes on a search. It magnetizes what you are looking for and how you begin to see the world. That's sacred.

So, while you make these principles a part of your story, you will have a far healthier and more rewarding life. These principles become a recycling dynamic so that while you are inspired and guided by these guiding benchmarks you will be entering your own best request of life.

Steve,

These are guideline principles. Add to them. Make them apply to your story. They help! How do I

know? It's because I keep trying them all along the way and find that they do, in fact, help. Make them yours and you will know what kind of difference they make for you!

Granddad

FACING REALITY

Question. When we talk about the tremendous opportunity we have in our time, are we in denial about how bad things are in the world, and on the streets of our cities? Crime is pervasive. Murders and suicides. Drugs and drug wars. Gang wars. Suicide bombings. Sex exploitation. Big business making big money on media and videos of violence, with little or no regard for how it is tearing down the highest ideals of our social fabric. On and on. Just read the paper or watch the news. Note all the greed, and all the unfair big money interests. It can be very discouraging and can increase the difficulties and risks we all face. Yet, in spite of the wrongs all around us, there are so many people who still live out a story of honor and hope in the midst of so much that is wrong. It becomes an uphill story, one's own outside Eden success story. They become the world's finest heroes.

When we hear stories about priests, ministers, politicians, business leaders, celebrities, people we looked up to and trusted, who have betrayed their leadership position and violate the principles of decency and respect, we are especially disappointed. And when TV entertainment-preachers make religion into a big show, and live lavish lifestyles by promising prosperity to those who will become their partners by pledging big dollars, it is a betrayal of the worst kind. All of these are stories of fallen heroes.

There have to be better ways. There are. There are choices we can make in spite of fallen heroes. We can still make the Principles of Problem Solving and the Big Ten Universal Qualities the backdrop against which we define who we are! We can intentionally choose nobility and honor, discipline and integrity, tolerance and respect as our place in the story. These form a framework in which we can choose to strengthen the good by lessening the bad. Even though we need millions who will make this their identity focus, it begins with a choice, one person at a time. The voice of wisdom calls each of us to follow the best we can be, especially in disappointing times.

Some problems can be solved only when they get big enough and tough enough that they finally get our real attention, and make us willing to enter the extra effort necessary to change them. That's why failure has the potential to be our teacher - why, finally we get it, and are ready to listen. Problems are big enough now. Opportunity is at hand.

In our digital-information age, we are at a pivotal point. This is not a time to forget our dreams and hopes - it's a time to reach for them as never before. It's time to talk about an overarching dream in which we keep on doing what we can to make a better world. Fortunately, millions of people buy into this model and live it out. They are life's heroes. They are the ones who set and reset their dreams. Together these become a collective force for good. These are the ones who advance Solomon's proverbs of how to be wise, and advance a new age of enlightenment. *The diligent man makes good use of everything he finds.* Proverbs 12:27

When Charles Dickens wrote his *Tale of Two Cities* he said, "It was the best of times; it was the worst of times." But for us, the question is not, "Which is it?" so much as "Which one am I trying to make it?" In our "tale of two tomorrows" what will I choose for my place in the story? Will I dare to choose ten uphill words that help? Will I give my best dreams their best chance to happen?

We can follow the principle of unrelenting persistence that Og Mandino sets forth as a positive affirmation in his book, *The Greatest Salesman in the World.*

Henceforth, I will consider each day's effort as but one blow of my blade against a mighty oak. The first blow may cause not a tremor in the wood, nor the second, nor the third. I will persist until I succeed. Each blow of itself, may seem trifling, and seem of no consequence. Yet from childish swipes the oak will eventually tumble. So it will be with my efforts today. . . I will persist until I succeed.[9]

Steve,

Here's a little metaphorical story I wrote recently about problem solving. I don't want you to try to figure out who "Jim" is in the story - just that he represents many people who reach for success in the face of challenge and find a way to turn problems into opportunity.

Granddad

It was the annual Thanksgiving Day dinner at the church. The leader was asking people to tell what they were thankful for. He turned to Jim and said, "Jim, would you tell what you are thankful for?"

"What?" Jim said. "You want to hear my story? Again? Most of you have heard it, but I would love to tell it. Again.

Five years ago I was in a wheel chair for the first time in my life. Eighty years old and one fall, and there I was, in the hospital, in a whole new situation.

In my mind, I can still hear the narrow tires on the wheel chair making a kind of hushed squeaky sound on the waxed floors of the hospital, as a nurse's aid pushed me out to the waiting area. My old suitcase sat on my lap. "Wait here for a moment," he said. "Social services is finishing up some paperwork and will take over from here."

---

[9] Og Mandino. The Greatest Salesman In The World. Bantam Books 1974

As I sat there, waiting, I became aware that I had been parked beside a man in his sixties, or so it seemed. He was sad. And I was sad. Here I was at eighty, and on my way to a nursing home! The social services director said that I could no longer live at home by myself. One fall, and now this.

I decided to speak to the man next to me. "You look as lonely as I feel," I said. "You coming in, or going home?" I asked.

"Going home?" he said as a question that revealed his shear consternation. "I have no home to go to now! It was foreclosed and padlocked four days ago, so I have been on the street since. The reason I am in here is because it's warm in here. That's all. But that's that much. I don't know what I am going to do. No family. No job. No money. No place to go and nothing much to do. I just thought of a line in a poem - don't even know where it comes from. Not sure exactly how it goes, but it talks about being down on your luck, and says, "do something for somebody, quick." Wish I knew what that is. I'd do it."

"Well, you just did," I said.

"Did?" he questioned, "I didn't do anything. I am just sitting here where it's warm."

I said, "What you did was make me feel better about my plight. You don't even have a home, and I have one. But, of course, they won't let me live there by myself any more. Strange how those factors have just come together while we are sitting here side by side as two strangers." I paused a moment. He sat in silence. Then I said, "I just got an idea! Maybe you could go home with me and live there and help take care of me, so I could live in my home, and you'd have a place to live. That would take care of both our problems. It's a wild idea. Of course, they'd never let that happen," I said. But when I paused and pondered a moment, I said,, " Or would they?"

The Social Services person came over with papers in her hand and said, "Okay, Jim. We are ready to go." That's when I said, "Miss, could you give me a few minutes to talk to my friend? Alone?"

"All right," she said. "I'll be back in a moment."

"What's your story?" I said, as I turned toward the stranger beside me.

"I lost my job," he said. "Said they didn't need me now. At sixty-one,

couldn't find another job. I spent all my savings. I couldn't make the payments on my house, so they evicted me. Now, here I am - on the streets in the daytime and staying at the shelter at night. That way I get two meals, and a place to sleep. But that won't last long. I have looked for a job for the last three days. For many years, I worked as a cook at a country club, but now I can't even find a job cooking burgers at McDonalds. Must be my age. But I know one thing, I could still cook if I just had a job!"

I turned to him and said, "You said, 'do something for somebody, quick.' How about if both of us did that? What if you went home with me and cooked for me? I need someone to live with me and do all the things which would make it possible for me to live at home, where I can afford it, instead of at a nursing home, where I can't afford it, at least not for very long. You need a place to live. I need a place to continue to live. What if we teamed up? If I helped you, you could help me. How's that for an idea? If it doesn't work out, we wouldn't know it until after we tried it."

That's my Thanksgiving story. That's our story, mine and Jim's. He went home with me. Been five years now. He takes care of me. I have a place to live and he has a place to live. Not only did he "do something for somebody quick," he did something that has lasted for five great years. That's what I am thankful for on this Thanksgiving Day.

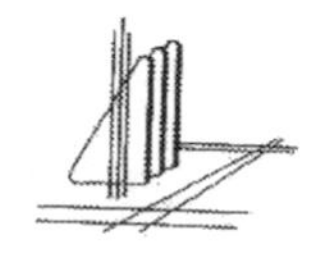

Chapter Eight

New Choices of Heroes

If you must choose, take a good name
rather than great riches;
for to be held in loving esteem is
better than silver and gold. Proverbs 22:1

Without wise leadership, a nation is in trouble. Proverbs 11:14

Choosing worthy and honorable heroes for our models is a necessary part of building a better future.

A better future is made by better people.

Steve,

These little notes I keep inserting make it seem like we are talking together against a backdrop of the farmhouse porch. I am enjoying it. Thanks again for asking me to do this. This has put my writings

in a whole new perspective. My hope is that all of this is helpful in your environmental science studies.

Granddad

THE RED BRICK SCHOOL I ATTENDED AS A BOY WAS HEATED BY A COAL fired furnace. Every morning the janitor had to take the ashes and cinders out of the furnace. He took them out into an area behind the auditorium, between the two wings of the building, and dumped them. Over time they built up a small hill. It was there we played king of the mountain. Of course, the biggest and strongest were the ones who could stay on top and be king longer than anyone else. Whoever could stay on top was considered a hero.

In life, sometimes the big and strong become heroes. It was that way when David's predecessor became king. Saul was chosen because he was one of the tallest men of his time. He was known as a mighty warrior. When David became king, he was not as big, but he was a mighty warrior. But when David's son, Solomon, became king, he wanted to be a different kind of king. He wanted to be known for his wisdom.

In our time, we are in urgent need of heroes who go beyond being big and strong, beyond big name celebrities, or beyond being great military people - we need heroes who are wise about how to live the good life. Our best heroes are those who personify the best qualities the human family has developed over the centuries. They are 'king of the mountain' because they are people of courage, kindness, caring, friendship, and respect - people whose minds and commitments to service make them models of integrity and nobility - people worthy of a Nobel prize, even if they are never celebrated as heroes on life's big stages. They are respected because they develop the best they can be, then give the best they have in their own unique time and place in history.

When we look back on the story of Solomon, we discover a major paradigm shift in the concept of the hero. It was a shift from the war hero to the wisdom hero.

David saw himself as the great warrior hero. He sent his armies out again and again, and often led them in battle. In spite of inflicting suffering and loss, sorrow and tears, injustice and hurt, they surged ahead cruelly, winning battles, conquering neighboring nations, imposing taxes on them, plundering their valuables and bringing back their finest young people as slaves.

Solomon had an army and kept horses and chariots ready to enter into battle, but he saw himself as a new hero who wouldn't need these because he followed the ways of wisdom, without waging war.

For David, God was the warrior God. Symbolically, God led his chosen nation in battle and conquest. One way this understanding was dramatized was to take their symbol of God's presence, the Ark of the Covenant, with them into battle.

But for Solomon, God was personified as Wisdom. People could serve God better by using their intelligence, and making wise choices which lead to a good life.

For David, success meant conquering vast territories and controlling them with occupation armies to expand his nation and power.

But for Solomon, the "invade and conquer" paradigm of his father was ending. He introduced the hero of cooperation with other nations. Instead of fighting against enemies, his nation could trade with them. That led to their building a fleet of ships for trade with the nations surrounding the Mediterranean Sea, as far away as the east coast of Africa. Also, there were land caravans that came regularly to Canaan as a trade destination. Solomon liked nice things - gold, silver, spices, special foods, and fine clothes. Through trading he could have these. As a result he became wealthy and enjoyed items of luxury that trade made possible.

Solomon ventured upon major building programs, not only in

the capital city, but in outlying areas, building fortress walls around several cities. Instead of conquering more territory, he protected what he had. There were chariot cities at strategic border locations, with big stables for hundreds of horses and chariots. To support all this expansion there was a massive refinery at Ezion-Geber, near the seaport on the Gulf of Aquabah. It was part of an industrial complex with smelters for refining copper and iron. Some of this was used within the kingdom, but much of it was a part of Solomon's expanding trade with other nations.

In a parallel to our time, we are seeing how collaboration through trade can be a means to advance a network of goods and services which can lessen the need to fight against others. The more we trade and share as a cooperative, interdependent world community, the fewer military confrontations we are likely to have. Care and share. It is a foundational concept for a wise and sustainable future.

Just as Solomon put David's war years of conquest behind him, and an era of cooperation and trade before him, so it is time for us to put the abusive conflicts of war behind us, and put a larger vision and paradigm of cooperation as a world family in front of us. We have a unique time in history to change from bomb diplomacy to collaboration and trade diplomacy. One hundred years from now, will we still be fighting wars, and with ever more sophisticated instruments of technology, or will we have found better ways to solve human conflicts under a larger identity umbrella of being one collaborative world family working together? Will we bridge the world's Olympic Games into Olympic Diplomacy? These are pivotal questions of great importance for our time in history. We need heroes who have big hearts, caring hands, integrity in thinking, and networks for working together for a better future!

There are nations which, instead of draining off their human and material resources in war, measure by their quality of life and are celebrated for superlatives such as having higher average income, better healthcare, better athletes, better education in science and mathematics, a greater interest in the humanities, cleaner air, fewer divorces, fewer people in prisons. In like manner, any nation will rise to its best when its people can be celebrated as the most noble citizens of the world because they define themselves by humanity's slowly distilled Big Ten Universal Qualities - the personal qualities of kindness, caring, honesty, and respect, the social relationship qualities of collaboration, tolerance, fairness, and integrity, and the summit of qualities, diplomacy and nobility.

While conflicts in our time, created by rebellious groups or nations, may require a strong military to defend a homeland, or to defend freedom in other parts of the world, the leading image and identity of a great nation need not be that it muscles its way in the world by its great military power.

Our own military is beginning to incorporate a shift in its identity and role in the world toward being peace keepers and peacemakers. In a new paradigm of creating a better future, our military array of equipment and personnel can be deployed anywhere in the world to provide valuable assistance in hurricanes, tsunamis, tornadoes, earthquakes, floods, diseases, fires, or other major disasters. Warships can become extensions of the concept embodied in the hospital ship, USS COMFORT, sailing to the ports of the world on missions of caring, healing, and reconciliation. Soldiers can be emissaries of peace and act in the roles similar to the Peace Corp to spread goodwill, expand education, share technical support, and advance health and cultural exchanges. Military leaders can defend both their own country and the greatest causes of human cooperation, imaging themselves as peacemakers and new heroes who are seeking to win the hearts and minds of people.

We may still choose to honor the courage and sacrifices so nobly made by military heroes, at the same time that we keep on reaching beyond war to finally to achieve the hero dream of Isaiah, who envisioned a time when "They shall beat their swords into plowshares, and their spears into pruning hooks; nation shall not lift up sword against nation, neither shall they learn war any more." Isaiah 2:4 RSV Such a dream is not for just one segment of the world family, but for all who want to be a part of humanity's greatest future story. Alternatives which make war a relic of the past are at hand now, awaiting for all of us to choose a larger identity in which we live as world citizens!

The new future hero is a patriot to more than just his own country. There is no conflict in flying, both the flag of one's own country, and a flag which represents the overarching dreams of all humanity being united in peace and cooperation. We best serve our own nation when we serve the best interest of all nations, united in the betterment of the earth family.

On May 12, 2008, a massive earthquake devastated the Sichuan Province of China and killed more than sixty-seven thousand people. The United States military flew in water, tents, generators, chain saws, and blankets to help the people recover from the destruction.

In the same year, the U S military stood ready to send in massive humanitarian aid following the cyclone, Nargis, which hit Myanmar (Burma) on May 3, causing eighty thousand deaths and displacing hundreds of thousands from their homes. A U S ship sailed to the coast and stood ready to send in military personnel, and fly in food, water, blankets, mosquito netting and plastic sheeting. Even though the Burmese government did not allow that aid, the U S military was ready to be a major force with massive humanitarian aid - ready to be heroes of a higher humanity.

Then, when a 7.0 magnitude earthquake demolished Port-au-Prince in Haiti in January of 2010, the aid for rescue and recovery was immediate and extensive.

On March 11, 2011. a 9.0 earthquake struck Japan, followed by a devastating tsunami and nuclear power plant failure. The U S military was there to help.

In any year that the Summer Olympics or the Winter Olympics

are staged anywhere in the world, they become a stage on which the world tests its search for the finest and best of human skills in terms of SWIFTER, HIGHER, STRONGER. The whole world is a stage where, not only athletes, but each person's story becomes a kind of Olympic game which tests, not just physical excellence, but how our best qualities can result in a new level of human relations and worldwide peaceful cooperative enterprises. We live in an unparalleled time of opportunity to light that flame, and fly that flag, which models a higher humanity. And whether or not any of us ever wins a hero's gold medal, we can try in our own way to live out the nobility of a world citizen and model the hero of the promise of the future right where we live.

Volunteer efforts by the Civilian Response Corps add to this shift toward working together to reach new levels of worldwide helpfulness, by sharing vital professional help in strategic locations in times of crisis. They offer services which utilize skills as doctors, lawyers, engineers, police officers, etc, to add to the peaceful relations in trouble spots. These same roles were the ones our military found to be important to carry out, alongside its combat operations, in Iraq.

A nation's strongest muscle should not come from weapons, but from policies and words that heal the past, clarify the present, and define the promise of a better future.

We are engaged in one of the greatest ideological contests of all history. We need the warriors of ideals and enduring qualities, who make noble sacrifices to defend the future against the destructive forces of greed, reckless uses of nature's resources, and intolerance toward others who are of different race, religion, and culture. We need the hero who defends, not only homelands, but the heartland of the earth family.

We have the tools of peaceful solutions not available in any other time. The instruments of communication are ubiquitous. The forums for conflict resolution can be assembled at strategic locations anywhere in the world on short notice. The United Nations is a standing forum for collaboration. Economic and political alliances can be a means to add new incentives for finding alternative solutions. Military budgets can be adjusted to include humanitarian enterprises. The worldwide community of scientists is beginning to address our global challenges at a new level of consciousness. The religious communities have an unparalleled opportunity to define their mission as humanitarian, rather than theological - as real world, rather than ethereal world, as here, rather than hereafter. What is needed is an identity template which pulls the world's people together in support of this larger understanding of our oneness of common cause as world citizens!

It can take time to reposition a nation's role, but the beginning point is in the thoughts and proverbs which define us. As never before, we have the opportunity to honor the heroes of wisdom and unity who help us become one family on earth, working together with all the tools of science, technology and the word tools of an overarching faith to advance the greatest era of peace and prosperity the world has ever known. It's the new sacred. It's an identity of choice where, *"If you must choose, take a good name rather than great riches; for to be held in loving esteem is better than silver and gold." Proverbs 22:1*

Let the hero of that ideal and noble vision stand tall among us. Let that hero be celebrated in our schools from kindergarten to college, in our research labs, in our churches, shrines, synagogues, mosques, in our halls of justice, in our legislative assemblies, in our books and magazines, in our television programs and movies, in our work and recreation. The hero who lives out humanity's best defining qualities is our greatest hero.

In our age of communications, world economics, internet, distance learning, text messaging, world travel, international sports events, collaboration among the world's scientists, global interests in climate concerns, space launches, and borderless energy needs, it is time for us to define our future in terms of how the world family can work together to maximize our potential to be the greatest people in the whole story of civilization!

To build this identity, we need help from many sources, especially today's media industry. In many ways, media inputs the mind with images which define our heroes and models. This is a time of great opportunity for media to enter a new responsible leadership role to celebrate the qualities of a higher humanity as an identity template for our most noble heroes.

An increasingly large segment of the media audience is more than ready for this. So many are tired of programming which elevates conflict, debases honor, de-humanizes women, demonizes people in vitriolic words, betrays integrity, elevates sensuality, and abuses respect. This audience is tired of violence and terrorism as entertainment - tired of violence that ignores tenderness, respect, and human dignity. They are hungry for something better. The media industry can turn this readiness into a great new opportunity!

What is happening is that the hero personalities in so much of current television and movies play so close to the edge of sensation, danger, and violence, that they get sucked in by it, and end up in the hospital, deranged, failures in business and social relationships, drug addicts, in prison for life, or dead. They live beyond the creative edge. They live in the disaster zone.

Out in real life, people with these behaviors end up with broken lives, in prison, addicted to drugs, or on the streets as losers. Some may even be celebrities and millionaires, but without respect or honor, they are huge failures. They may be celebrated briefly by others with equal loser thinking, but they are not heroes. When this scenario is played out, the story can be written in one word - failures - failures who let themselves and all their teammates down. They live over the edge. They could have looked down the road and read the signs indicating tragedy ahead, then made alternative choices, and written entirely different stories - stories that simply honor the best qualities of our higher humanity on whatever stage life gives us for our place in the story.

When we update the Solomon thesis to our own time, we realize that we all have that "look ahead" capacity in the brain, ready to be used. Without it, we travel a blind journey. Some choose such blindness. The consequences can be disastrous. But, instead of roads to disaster, we can look ahead and make wise choices early, in childhood, in youth, in mainstream living, so that the future we ask for is one where we dream our best dreams and give them their best chance to happen, on location, in our story!

OUR GREATEST POWER

The power to choose is our greatest power. It's a gift of our DNA. Solomon personified this crossroad of choices in metaphors of two contrasting women, Wisdom, and the Harlot. In his book of *Proverbs*, he gives a vivid description of the enticements of the harlot. He tells how she is dressed and what cunning words she uses to entice her lovers into her bedroom, where the silk sheets are fragrant and soft. Her appeal is alluring, and many young men are drawn in by her flattery and promises, only to pay in regret later.

In a contrasting metaphor, Solomon portrays Wisdom as the lady who calls upon young men to think their way past the pitfalls of following the harlot, so they can enter a request of life that rewards good choices. That's the winner in life! *He who loves wisdom loves his own best interest and will be a success.* Proverbs *19:8*

Pointing to flaws in the media industry is not to condemn, but to identify what can be better. Some good changes are already happening. There is an increase in credible programs which connect entertainment with learning and wholesome living, based in scientific knowledge and our best defining qualities. Programs are being presented which define good solutions to current problems. Leading characters are shown to be heroes with character and integrity, and who define a great tomorrow instead of defending old yesterdays, or celebrating humanity's highest common denominators, not it's lowest. These changes are welcomed. More are needed. Slowly, but now more rapidly than in a thousand years before, we are advancing to an era of a more wholesome identity for our heroes.

Our best hero personifications rise above categories of race, nationality, religion, or gender. What matters is that they model intelligence, honor, integrity, unity, and confidence - heroes who are so self assured they are not afraid to exemplify the simple qualities of being kind, considerate, helpful, and collegial - models of nobility who lead the way to a wholesome sustainable identity for a better tomorrow.

So the challenge and opportunity for the media industry is to give us stories that both entertain and inform - stories which reflect the new sacred, expand the molecular knowledge base, and inspire and awaken the potential in ourselves to reach for the better side of our humanity.

In our time we have a wide variety of heroes. They are popularly represented in magazines with a specialized focus. I decided to go down to Barnes and Noble and survey the extensive range of magazines which highlight today's variety of heroes.

Wow! What a selection! Many highlight heroes who model physical skills, all the way from weight lifting by sheer muscle power, to those who achieve skills in multiple sports, highlighted in *Pro Football, Car and Driver, Tennis, Golf Digest.* Other magazines extend the focus on heroes of celebrity, style, music, and wealth, *People, Glamour, Classic Rock, Fortune 500.* The list could go on and on.

Science magazines have dedicated several pages to the work of a team of heroes, whose collective knowledge and skills have landed the Phoenix Lander and Curiosity on the surface of Mars, one hundred and seventy million miles away from Earth.

Whether in one specific magazine, or highlighted in all of our magazines, we need pictures, narrative, exposition, and stories which focus on the heroes who model a higher humanity, manifested in the personal qualities of the Big Ten, kindness, caring, honesty, and respect, advanced in our social relationships of collaboration, tolerance, fairness, integrity, and elevated in a reach for diplomacy and nobility. These are the valued qualities which can take our human story up to new levels of excellence, worthy of us in our time in history. These expand our vision and build our best dreams. These give our best dreams their best chance to happen!

The best hero in the information age is no longer only the brave cowboy type, the decorated military leader, the super rich empire builder, the latest stage star, or popular religious leader, but the new hero who dares to test life's most admirable qualities on the changing landscape of today's multiple settings. Our need is greater than ever before for heroes who achieve a high humanity, unique to each person's time and place in the story.

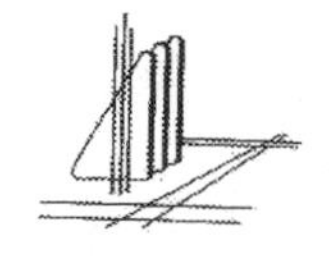

CHAPTER NINE

The Dream and Opportunity

These are the proverbs of King Solomon of Israel.
He wrote them to teach his people how to live -
how to act in every circumstance.

Determination to be wise is
the first step to becoming wise. Proverbs 4:7

Never forget to be truthful and kind. Proverbs 3:3

A merry heart doeth good like medicine. Proverbs 15:13

I would have you learn this great fact:
that a life of doing right is the wisest life there is. Proverbs 4:11

We live in a great time of opportunity
to answer some of life's big questions
which define our place in the story.

Steve,

Sooner or later we all leave a legacy. It was said of one person's legacy, 'He went about doing good.' We often refer to him with continuing respect as the Master Teacher. Our unsurpassed opportunity in our time is to learn forward as we go about doing good.

Granddad

A QUESTION ON THE COVER OF ONE ISSUE OF SEED, A LEADING SCIence magazine, asked in bold letters, **"Can Science Save The American Dream?"** [10]

The question is superimposed on a picture of the landscape of the Moon. In the center of the picture, an American flag is planted in the soil and its shadow falls on the lunar landscape. The picture was taken on July 20, 1969, by Buzz Aldrin when Apollo ll landed on the moon. That event represents a milestone of achievement in the history of man's development and exploration between the stone age and the space age. The question on the cover of SEED is of great importance at this time in our information-technology age. But the question about saving the American dream needs to be expanded to ask, **"Do science and religion need to build a partnership to help save the human family dream?"**

We wonder, if after thousands of years of tradition, now splintered into a thousand different factions, religion has done much more than divert human efforts into perpetuating it's own existence at the expense of the human family's good. It's focus has been too much on transcendence and not enough on immanence. It's time for religion and science to build a new partnership.

[10] SEED. October 2007

Far too long religion has distanced itself from the growing insight provided by science. Religion has made transcendence and heavenly bliss the goal of human life, instead of immanence and a reach for the best life possible in a real world. So, our first response to the question about the help of religion to partner in the human dream, is one of serious doubt.

However, in our digital information age, and with a growing understanding of the oneness of all molecular existence, the sun may be rising on a new day in which there could be such a partnership. A paradigm shift is needed on the part of both religion and science. The human family has its greatest opportunity ever to move from an authority-based religion to a knowledge-based faith. The world family has its greatest opportunity ever to use its tremendous advance in the tools of technology to build the "better angels of our nature." Together, we can update our understanding of the God of all molecular existence and refocus our mission on building a better humanity. The sunrise on such a partnership may be dawning.

Religion bears a great responsibility for this change. For too long, religion has looked back more than forward, and studied itself, and reconstructed and refined its own self-protective views instead of building a vision of a greater humanity. Out of that protective self-interest, it has been intellectually dishonest, persecuted its scientists, banned and burned leading-edge books, and held people in captivity to tradition by fear, rather than emancipate people to learn about the nature of our existence and about real time humanity. As religion gradually moves to a new paradigm of human identity outside that restrictive bondage to the traditions of the past, a slow move toward a budding partnership with science and technology may finally be occurring.

As this larger identity umbrella expands, religion has a unique opportunity to help its followers build a more inclusive identity of 'we the earth family' instead of 'us;' and 'them,' in little enclaves of defensive units. Under this larger identity framework, we can recognize many faiths, or no faith at all, as part the human family's larger umbrella of identity, where the goal and potential is to think and act as world citizens.

Some problems are solvable only when they get big enough. Not only are our problems now of that magnitude, our perspectives have changed so that we now see the human family's future as a whole on the planet, where we either learn to live together, or fail to reach our best tomorrows. We have learned, from natural disasters, from environmental concerns, from space age explorations, and from global networking information flow to widen our identities.

We have also come to that place in history where we realize that our faith needs to be an overarching framework that embraces many sub-identities under a larger umbrella of being world citizens in common cause.

After serving a full career as a minister, I entered a new test arena in which I worked just as a human being, outside the cloak of religious identity. I worked as a sales associate in the suit department of a major department store. There my expectation of myself was that I would simply live out a basic world citizen identity - that I would require of myself that I live up to the model of treating all persons by the gold standard of the Big Ten Universal Qualities, outside of any religious, political, or cultural label. I tried to respond to rich and poor, religious or non-religious, learned or unlearned alike, across all our ethnic and cultural spectrum, with kindness, cordiality, and respect. My goal was to be inclusive, tolerant, and understanding of all people, just as one human being to another, beyond all differences.

Not just at our places of work, but wherever we have a place in the story, each of us has our own unique opportunity to be a world class citizen. We can live each day with cordiality, honesty, warmth, respect, kindness, and generosity - traveling not so much to some other place in the world, as being our best on location - on university campuses, at the check-out at the grocery store, among family, friends, and neighbors, at church, at the club, at civic gatherings, at work, on the phone, the internet, - wherever we share the stage with others who like to be treated with respect, kindness, and congeniality.

When these qualities are incorporated into our lives, we will be more successful at home, among friends, and in our careers. People like us most when we manifest our best defining qualities. We learn as we try, and grow as we learn. And if, and when, we fail, we know what we must do to restore our own credibility - reach again. King Solomon knew that. He said, "*Don't you know that the good man, though you trip him up seven times, will each time rise again?" Proverbs 24:16*

When we move the question about saving American dream, or the human dream, down to a personal identity level, the question becomes, "Can I combine the tools of science and technology together with the best universal defining qualities into my story? Can I help advance the human story to the next level up of a higher humanity?

The classic story of Dr Albert Schweitzer is a model for that kind of world citizenship.

At a young age, Albert Schweitzer was a philosopher, physician, celebrated organist, theologian, clergyman, organ builder, and an authority on the life and works of Johann Sebastian Bach. But at age thirty, he decided to become a medical student and then go to Africa to be a doctor. He said, "It struck me as incomprehensible that I should be allowed to lead such a happy life, while I saw so many people around me wrestling with care and suffering." His own words describe the resulting decision. "One brilliant summer morning at Gunsbach, … there came to me as I awoke, the thought that I must not accept this happiness as a matter of course, but must give something in return for it. Proceeding to think this matter out at once with calm deliberation, while the birds were singing outside, I settled with myself before I got up, that I would consider myself justified in living till I was thirty for science and art, in order to devote myself from that time forward to the direct service of humanity."[11]

It was a compelling identity shift. Upon completion of his medical education, at age thirty-eight, he went to Lambarene, French Equatorial Africa to serve as a medical missionary. In recognition of that service to humanity, in 1952 he was awarded the Nobel peace prize and, in turn, used the money from that distinguished award to expand the hospital he had built in Africa. He modeled being a world citizen, and has been called one of the greatest Christians of his time.

Millions, whose names will never be known beyond their local communities where they march in the world citizen parade without any special recognition, can be among the world's heroes and models.

When we measure the way we live by the universal defining qualities, a healing takes place inside. We feel wholesome. We respect ourselves. A new kind of confidence guides our emotions and empowers us to go for honor and wholeness of mind and body. Over time, sometimes after much trial and error, we become the person we define ourselves to be. With new feelings of confidence and generosity, we realize we always have something to give - some act of kindness, some word of encouragement, some expression of positive attitude. In social settings, in academic circles, in business sessions, in family gatherings, we can respond to various situations out of the honest and confident feelings created by our identity of being true to our chosen Big Ten Universal Qualities. When this is our quest, it's amazing how good it makes us feel about ourselves and how it builds confidence and releases our best and most open social graces. We have less temptation to brag about our success, or position ourselves in a kind of quick facade. We have no need for drugs or alcohol to lower inhibitions to enhance our social skills - we are already self-programmed to be generous

[11] Albert Schweitzer. Mentor Books. 1949 NY

in friendship, respectful of others, gracious, congenial, courteous, and fair, and above all, to be kind. In the continual reentering and reinforcing of this defining template, we will gradually reprogram the brain on the side of the "better angels of our nature." This quest for our higher fulfillment is sacred. It's not far from what Solomon indicated by saying, *"I would have you learn this great fact: that a life of doing right is the wisest life there is." Proverbs 4:11*

Steve,

My confident feelings about a better future and being better people is not based on the past but on the future we can achieve, little by little, when we simply try to reach for "the wisest life there is." I know that in your environmental studies and future plans, we are on that same journey of faith and hope. Unique to our place in the story, we both want our own parallel to the Albert Schweitzer story.

Granddad

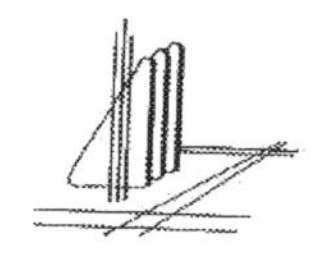

CHAPTER TEN

A Home for Us

He who troubles his household will inherit the wind. Proverbs 11:29 RSV

"I want those already wise to become the wiser and become leaders by exploring the depths of meaning in these nuggets of truth." Proverbs 1:5,6

Planet Earth can continue to be a great home for us, but it's up to us.

We are all indebted to the past, but we are even more indebted to the future.

The best way to honor the past is to build a better future.

Steve,

Considerable age separates us, but we travel parallel journeys.

We must never forget the progress humanity has made to get to this age of unparalleled potential, and we must be sure it doesn't stop with us. We are the future. We are only one, but we are one - on a quest to help make earth a home into lengthening new tomorrows.

Thanks for asking me to share this journey through this manuscript. It is a high honor and privilege.

Granddad

BEFORE THE QUEEN OF SHEBA CAME TO VISIT WITH KING SOLOMON and to share proverbs with him, she may have heard the widely circulated story about his wisdom, when two mothers brought their case for him to decide.

One of the mothers was holding a crying baby in her arms.

The other mother held a still and lifeless child in her arms. That mother was crying. With tears rolling down her anguished face, she pleaded, "Your honor, my king, we were both sleeping with our children in the same bed. While that other mother was asleep, she rolled over on her baby and it died. When she discovered what had happened, she placed the lifeless baby beside me and took my baby. When morning came I saw that the baby was not mine. Now she claims that the dead child is mine and that the living baby is hers. O my king, please say that she must give me back my baby."

The other mother pushed forward, holding the living baby in her arms. She said, "This is my precious baby. She wants to take it from me. She claims it is hers. But it's not. She's lying. Her tears are false. She is just trying to impress you. This is my baby."

Solomon stood there looking at the two mothers, each holding a baby, one living, and one lifeless. Solomon turned to a guard and said, "Let me borrow your sword." Then he turned to the mother holding the living baby and said, "Let me have the baby. I'll just cut it in two pieces and each of you can have a half."

Quickly the other mother rushed up, pleading, "Oh, no. No! Please! Please, my king! Please, do not do that. Let her have the baby. She can have it. Just let the baby live."

Solomon handed the sword back to the guard, and said, "Give the baby to this mother who could not even think of killing the baby. She's the real mother."

In our time we would have solved that dilemma with technology. We would have called for a DNA test. But that was then, and this is now, and the road between had a long way to go before getting up to our time in the age of knowledge, with its increasing array of technological developments and tools.

The advances of technology in even a few years in our time, far surpasses those of a thousand years earlier, or even a hundred years, and the developments continue to grow at an unprecedented rate. It's all part of what we are inheriting by being a part of the greatest age in history. So we need to ask, "Are we are developing the 'wisdom of Solomon' at a rate equal to our advancements in technology?" It is a pivotal question. Whether or not we are doing that, we can! If we can, that is a responsibility that rests on our shoulders to do what we can to keep our faith current with the progression of knowledge. Only by trying to do that can we have intellectual integrity. It is our sacred responsibility!

On the knowledge-based side of the great divide, the more we incorporate the overarching, universal, defining qualities of the Big Ten into our identity and resulting choices, the more likely we are to build a partnership of religion and science with a wisdom that honors our place in the molecular age and our time of unfinished dreams.

As I was near the completion of this book, I drove up to Doughton Park by way of the scenic Blue Ridge Parkway in the mountains of North Carolina. I would be spending the night at Bluffs Lodge. After I checked in, I walked up to nearby Wildcat Rock overlooking Basin Cove, 550 feet below, so far down that a little log cabin down there looked like a little shoe box. The mountain peaks on each side are so steep that the little house was already in the shadow of the mountains to the west by mid afternoon. The pioneer log house in that deep canyon was once the home of Martin and Janie Caudill. In that little cabin, nestled in a small clearing in the trees at the head of the cove, they raised their fourteen children. About one mile down the creek, is where Martin's father lived in the Basic Cove community. The nearest settlement beyond that was eight miles farther down, reachable half by foot trail and half by road.

That little cabin still stands, evoking a sense of awe. When I was a daring college student, I went to that cabin, not by coming up the valley by road and foot trail, but down from the Wildcat Rock side, slipping and sliding down the steep side of the bluff. Then, quietly, and feeling like an invading stranger, I stooped and entered through its one door. At one end there was a loft where the Caudill family had slept. A big fireplace covered much of the space at the other end of that little log house. That sense of awe has been a part of my lingering memories of that visit with yesterday.

On my two day excursion to the mountains, now many years beyond those bold and daring college days, when I looked down from Wildcat Rock on that microcosm of history, I sat there on a rock wall ledge, reflecting on their place in the story in their time, and on my place in the story in my time.

The next morning I extended that contrast in time, as I drove about three miles east and stopped at the historic Martin and Caroline Brinegar log cabin, built around 1880, and where some of the family lived up to 1935. A garden, outhouse, smokehouse, cellar, and spring house were nearby. There they made a home, surrounded by miles and miles of tree-covered mountains and valleys. Their little world was part of an ongoing story where, night after night, the moon had reflected the sun, while stars, billions of miles beyond, twinkled in the nighttime sky, as time went by. The cabin is now on the National Historic Registry and open to visitors so they can reflect on their journey stories in contrast, or parallel.

I believe in, and respect, the yesterday of those two families, and honor their success as persons who survived and triumphed in the face of struggle and hardship. But I also believe in an overarching vision of tomorrow. I believe in better homes and gardens, better farms and cities, better cars and planes, in better dreams, and in better people. I believe in yesterday, but I believe even more in tomorrow, where we can take a place in our new technological fantasy land with integrity and honor, led by our finest defining qualities.

Is this vision of the future under threat? It doesn't have to be. We can make choices witch lead us into the crowning story of our human journey.

The little farm where I grew up is not on the National Historic Registry, like the Martin and Caroline Brenegar cabin. But when my place in the story becomes a memory, I hope that little farm can continue to be a part of the story for future generations, where they will connect with yesterday and nature, at the same time they connect with changing technology and new dreams of wise tomorrows. In such a parallel journey, quality of life is of greater value than advances in technology, and living better is more important than living longer. We can continue to live by the personal qualities of **kindness, caring, honesty,** and **respect,** leading up to the social relationship qualities of **collaboration, tolerance, fairness,** and **diplomacy,** and the summit qualities of **integrity,** and **nobility.**

Recently I went back to the little town where I lived as a boy. In those earlier days, I often rode my bicycle on the three mile journey from the country into the little storybook town. My dad had a garage on the west end of that unique town. On the other end of town was a big two-story house which was the home of one of the buggy factory owners of earlier days. That stately old house is still there. It is next door to the funeral home where both my mother and dad lay in state following their deaths. There, in the lobby of the funeral home, is one of the old buggies built in the buggy factory in that town. A lot of change has taken place since that old buggy was a mode of travel, and since I rode my bicycle on those streets as a boy. I read the proverbs of Solomon then. I read them now, updated as the Big Ten Universal Qualities, and reflect on life's journey.

My being back in my hometown was for a family visitation upon the death of my cousin, a lady of ninety-three. My memories reach back to my boyhood days and the big white frame country church where I first knew her, and where she was present every Sunday with her family.

As I reflect on that occasion, I can still hear the slightly out of tune piano at the church, and the voices of those noble country people, where my cousin was often sitting beside my mother, singing, "Bringing in the sheaves. We shall come rejoicing, bringing in the sheaves."

While I was writing at the farmhouse, that old song echoed in my memory. I stopped writing and went upstairs to the dark room, where I had gone before looking for an old book. There on that same mantle, where I had found *Hurlbut's Story of the Bible* earlier, I found an old book of songs with those metaphorical words.

> Sowing in the morning, sowing seeds of kindness,
> Sowing in the noontide and the dewy eve;
> Waiting for the harvest, and the time of reaping,
> We shall come rejoicing, bringing in the sheaves.

> Bringing in the sheaves, Bringing in the sheaves,
> We shall come rejoicing, bringing in the sheaves.[12]

At the funeral home that evening, I expressed my admiration for my cousin, as I shook hands with her three children, who now extend the legacy.

The religious paradigm of the church we attended was behind the times. But above and overarching that limited paradigm, big hearted people met there to share their faith that was up with the times because it was focused on the humanitarian qualities of the Big Ten Universal Qualities.

Our time in history and place in the story is part of a larger story. It is a part of the ongoing and mysterious processes of nature. It's part of the 13.82 billion year history of the cosmos. It is part of the four and half billion year history of planet Earth. It is part of the sixty thousand years of human history. And now, in our age of technology, we are privileged to be a part of that ongoing story. We are beginning to be more aware than ever of the importance of the story we are writing in our time and place in the earth and human story. When we read the proverbs of Solomon, we know that we are accountable for that story, and its extension for a thousand generations into the future.

As an unintended consequence of how big our human family has grown and its impact on mother earth, our anxiety over the changing environment has not only become a part of our daily conversations, we have begun to think more about the earth as our home. We are more aware than ever that we must make wise choices so it will continue to be a home for us in the vast cosmos. It is here that we are privileged to live as part of the boundless mystery of all molecular existence. We are a part of all that is, and it is a part of us. It's God is our God, and our God is its God. Whether or not we

[12] George A Minor

live on the greatest planet in the boundless cosmos, it is, in fact, a wondrous planet! It's where we live and have the opportunity to use all the planet's resources, natural, scientific, and human to write our story. That's all any of us ever get, or need, a place in the story. It's where we have the very special opportunity to live by the Big Ten Universal Qualities as our overarching identity framework and turn old endings into new beginnings as the future we ask for.

Dear Granddad,

I have now finished reading your manuscript on The Future We Ask For. My own future has been changed as a result. I have been seeing myself as an environmental scientist. You have helped me to see myself as more than that - to see myself as a citizen of the global earth family.

All through your draft manuscript, you entered notes to me which highlighted the importance of each section. These made it seem like we were dreaming together.

Now I have a question-suggestion for you as my valued mentor. Would it be possible for you to include your notes to me in your book when it is published? Perhaps there are a lot of "grandsons" in your reading audience who also could have the privilege of having a "granddad" who is also their mentor.

With deep gratitude and esteem.

Your Grandson

Steve

SEQUELS: New Tomorrows, Apple Blossom Time, The Future We Ask For, A Place In The Story, Eagles View Mountain, Sunrise Dreams, The New Sacred.